GLORIA

Katherine Shaw

For my Nannan Janet, who would have been so proud.

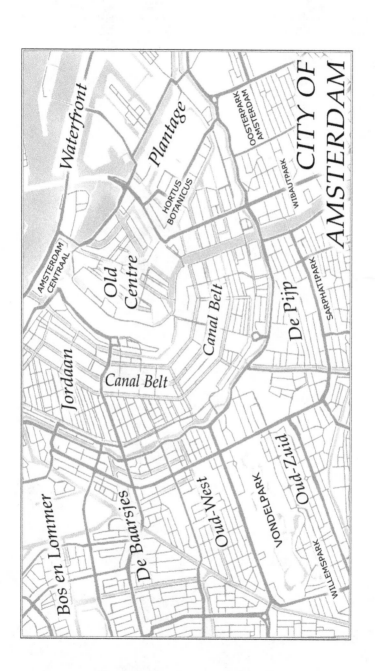

CITY OF AMSTERDAM

Waterfront

Plantage

OOSTERPARK AMSTERDAM

HORTUS BOTANICUS

AMSTERDAM CENTRAAL

WIBAUTPARK

Old Centre

Canal Belt

Canal Belt

De Pijp

SARPHATIPARK

Jordaan

Canal Belt

Oud-Zuid

Bos en Lommer

De Baarsjes

Oud-West

VONDELPARK

WILLEMSPARK

For sweetest things turn sourest by their deeds;
Lilies that fester smell far worse than weeds.

-William Shakespeare

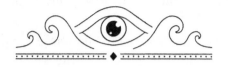

CHAPTER ONE

Gloria leaned against the cold railings of the Juliet balcony. Her eyes, as always, were drawn to the river, its shimmering surface snaking off towards the horizon. So close, and yet desperately out of reach. Bending forwards, the metal dug into her pale, freckled skin, almost to the point of pain, but it was worth it to breathe in that fresh, open air. She yearned to be on the sea, the wind whipping her long, red hair behind her as the salty spray licked her face. That wouldn't happen for a long time, now. Maybe it would never happen again. She knew she had to forget about the life she used to live and be content, but the water seemed to call to her. It beckoned her to come home.

Taking one last, deep breath, Gloria retreated into her bedroom and slid the balcony doors shut. Despite the light shining in through the wide, glass panes, the room felt dull and lifeless, and she felt a sudden urge to get out. She strode to the doorway, flinging the door back to try and let some air into a space that, despite its great size, felt almost suffocating.

Before she knew it, she was downstairs in the kitchen. She didn't even remember pouring the glass of wine, but as the silken red liquid slid down her throat, she felt soothed. She closed her eyes and, for a moment, she was outside her favourite bar, the canal by her side and the soft early evening sun caressing her face, without a care in the world.

'That's your second bottle already this week.'

Busted.

Gloria's eyes fluttered open. She was greeted once more by the stark, clinical whiteness of the kitchen counter. 'I hadn't realised you were counting,' she said, lifting her head to face her husband, who was home early again. She regretted her sharp tone as a look of hurt flashed across his handsome face.

'I'm just thinking of your health, dear,' Greg said, raising his eyebrows and offering a gentle smile which screamed good intentions.

'Okay, yes, sorry. I'll just have one glass today, I promise.' Gloria didn't want an argument. She rose, already turning towards the open back door. As the mild summer breeze stirred the loose hair around her shoulders, she felt drawn outside, to the space and sunlight. To nature. 'I'm going to paint.'

'Now?' Even with her back to him, Gloria knew Greg's face had dropped. 'I've just come in, can't you spend the evening with me?'

For a moment, she didn't move. She was stuck, forced again to choose between her creativity and the freedom it brought her, and her responsibility as a dutiful wife. She took a deep breath.

'You're right. Let me get started on dinner.'

◆——— • ● ◆ ● • ——— ◆

For all intents and purposes, Gloria had the perfect life. Greg made good money as a successful medical consultant, and he was happy for her to spend her days painting in their lush Surrey garden, rather than going out to work for an unnecessary second income. She could spend her days drifting through their spacious four-bedroom detached home, filling her hours however she pleased. So why didn't she feel happy?

At least here, in her studio, she found peace. Although Greg didn't understand her creative spirit whatsoever, he had granted her a wish she had dreamed of since she was a little girl – her own outdoor studio. He'd even let her help design it, with tall, rectangular windows letting in vast amounts of natural light, and wide doors which welcomed all the sights and sounds of the garden. It was idyllic, and Gloria found herself working in here more and more of late.

It was mid-afternoon, and the dipping sun provided the perfect backdrop to her latest painting, awash with the reds, oranges and yellows of the coming sunset. Losing herself in the brush strokes, Gloria felt an inner peace she seldom experienced anywhere else. She was fully absorbed in a daze of colours and sweeping shapes, the canvas coming alive as she danced the brush across its surface.

As time drew on, she resisted the urge to look at her phone, lying face down on a nearby cushion; if she didn't know the time, there was nothing else she should be doing. It didn't matter that she was covered in paint – she'd even got it in her hair this time – and she didn't need to put on any airs and graces; she could just be herself, and it felt wonderful.

Closing her eyes to picture the scene she was trying to replicate on the canvas, Gloria's mind was dragged back into reality by a sudden buzzing sound. One of these days, she'd remember to turn her phone off vibrate. It was no doubt just a message from Greg, letting her know he was on his way home or was running late at the office. When the phone continued to buzz, however, Gloria's interest was piqued. It was rare she got phone calls lately. Even Iris had started to stick to their weekly schedule now she was growing up, much to Gloria's disappointment. She missed her little girl.

Turning over the phone, Gloria frowned as she saw a name that, although very familiar, she hadn't seen in an awfully long time.

Katie.

It must have been months since they last spoke, maybe even a year or more. What could she possibly be calling for? Gloria almost didn't answer, wary of the potential awkwardness that comes with an extended lack of communication, but she didn't want to offend someone who must now be one of her only friends in the UK.

'Hello? Katie?' Gloria answered with some trepidation.

'Gloria! Long time no speak, right?' After the tranquillity of the garden studio, Katie's sudden burst of enthusiasm made Gloria jump a little. 'How's life in The Manor?'

Gloria couldn't help but chuckle at that. Katie was one of her few British friends who knew her from before she met Greg. When she had first seen the size of their marital home she had dubbed it "The Manor", and the name had stuck. Greg, of course, hated it.

'Um, yeah. Good, thanks.' Gloria started to relax. Why had she been so nervous of speaking to Katie? They had been extremely close in the past, after all. 'Nothing interesting to report back, I'm afraid. How have you been?'

As Katie chattered about her recent high-flying adventures in the world of marketing, Gloria sunk down onto the plump cushions which lined the interior wall of the studio. It felt good to hear her friend's voice again. Maybe she had been spending too much time on her own lately.

'Quick question for you, Glor.'

Gloria's mind snapped back to the present as she realised she might be expected to respond.

'Are you still painting?'

That was an odd question; no one seemed interested in Gloria's art these days. 'Yes. Most days, actually. It's good for the soul.'

Katie laughed at that – she had never been one for spirituality. 'That's what I was hoping to hear! Listen, let's not catch up over the phone. When are you next free for lunch? I'm in London this week, and I've got what I think is an exciting proposal for you!'

Gloria couldn't pinpoint exactly why, but her conversation with Katie had lifted her mood immensely, so much so that she found herself singing as she washed her hair to rid it of this afternoon's overenthusiastic brushstrokes. She didn't even care that the notes fell flat sometimes – she was out of practice, after all. In fact, she couldn't remember the last time she'd sung, whether privately or otherwise. She certainly didn't have the confidence to perform anymore. Those days were behind her.

Downstairs, Gloria's bare feet tapped softly as she scurried into the kitchen, still wrapped up in a bath sheet and singing quietly to herself. She even found herself sinking into a few of her old dance moves from her days in the club, spinning on the gleaming tiles and almost losing her balance.

'And just where have you been?'

Gloria started. She'd lost track of time completely, and was surprised to hear her husband's voice. She turned to face Greg, dressed impeccably in a perfectly tailored suit and sporting a dazzling smile.

'Oh, hi, darling,' Gloria said, as her heart rate settled. 'I was just washing my hair. Paint everywhere again!'

Greg strolled up to Gloria and wrapped one of her thick, red curls around his finger.

'You should be more careful,' he said softly, rubbing the hair between his fingers as if savouring the texture. 'You know how much I love your luscious locks.' He added with a wink.

It was true, Greg has always been enamoured with Gloria's hair. In fact, it was apparently what had first drawn him to her; he'd told her as much on their first meeting, back in Amsterdam.

'So, what's got you in this uncharacteristically cheerful mood?' he asked, his eyes lingering on the hair between his fingers before he finally let his hand drop and fixed his gaze on her face. 'I don't think I've heard you sing in months.'

'Nothing in particular. Although Katie called today, which was nice.'

Greg frowned, confusion settling on his face. 'Katie who?'

'Katie Embleton, my old friend from way back. She went off to do a business degree, but visited briefly when I first moved here. Remember?'

Greg's eyes seemed to flash for a second, but they returned to normal so quickly, Gloria wondered if she'd imagined it.

He let out a sharp laugh. 'Oh, the silly marketing girl? Damn, Gloria, I didn't think she'd interest you anymore.'

She was a little taken aback, but shrugged it off. She didn't understand Greg's sense of humour sometimes, but had learned to nod along with his jokes. 'Well, it's not like we're *close* anymore. And I was surprised to see her number flash up, to be honest.'

'She was probably just on the hunt for gossip, knowing her type. She's barking up the wrong tree if she's hoping for scandals in rural Surrey.' Greg turned towards the dining room, making a beeline for the waiting newspaper as if the conversation was already concluded.

'She's asked me to meet her for coffee in London tomorrow. I think it'll be nice to get out and about for a change.'

Greg stopped and turned, his face seeming to darken as he looked at Gloria, concern painted across his features. 'Are you sure that's a good idea?' At Gloria's obvious confusion he softened his face a little. 'It's been a while since you've been into the city – it isn't the way it used to be, you know. Someone as attractive and...*vulnerable* as you would be an obvious target for muggers, or worse.'

Gloria frowned, resisting the urge to roll her eyes. Greg could be so melodramatic. It was true she hadn't been into the city for a while, but could it really be that risky nowadays, at lunch time in the middle of the week? Katie had said she had an exciting proposal, and life had been one identical day after another for Gloria lately. Half the time she didn't even know what day it was. She would go crazy if she was trapped alone in this house for much longer.

'It would be good for me to get out, Greg,' she implored, throwing on her best puppy dog eyes. 'Besides, Katie will be with me, and she's always in London. She'll know where's safe to go.'

A faint crease of unease still plagued Greg's forehead, but he shrugged and offered up a small smile. 'You know I can't resist those sapphire eyes. All right, have fun, but be careful. And don't be too late home, okay?'

CHAPTER TWO

It was a perfect day for a trip to the city. The sky was almost cloudless, and the sun glinting off of the high-rise buildings made for quite the spectacle as the train slowly pulled into Waterloo Station. It had been so long since Gloria had been in a big city, and the hustle and bustle of London made her feel more at home than quiet, leafy Surrey had for quite some time. She missed the energy she gained from being around so many other people, an anonymous figure in the centre of a hive of activity. It was invigorating.

Katie was waiting for her at the station, apparently sharing Greg's distrust of Gloria's self-navigation skills. She looked resplendent, dressed all in black as if she had just stepped out of a high-powered board meeting. Gloria suppressed a flutter of nerves at seeing her old friend looking so sophisticated and successful – she hoped things wouldn't be weird between them.

'As much as I appreciate having a chaperone, I think you're forgetting I single-handedly wound my way through Europe back in the pre-smartphone era!' Gloria laughed.

Granted, Europe hadn't been easy sailing, but she had survived it, after all.

'I thought you might be a bit rusty, now you're Lady of the Manor.' Katie winked, looping her arm through Gloria's and leading her off into the crowded street.

In stark contrast to their old haunts of the past —usually whichever local bar offered the cheapest wine by the glass — Katie led Gloria to a chic new restaurant right on the Thames. Thankfully, she opted to travel by taxi, so Gloria didn't have to embarrass herself by struggling to walk in the heels she had dusted off for the occasion. As she took in her opulent surroundings, she found herself feeling relieved she had made the decision to dress smartly. Although, if she was honest with herself, she'd had so few excuses to dress up lately, she would have donned that same pretty summer dress if they'd been dining out at McDonald's.

'It's gorgeous here, isn't it?' Katie said, staring around at the glistening black and white surfaces and glittering crystal light fixtures. She seemed to be dressed to match her elegant surroundings, her simple but tasteful 'little black dress' matching the sleek decor perfectly. Her neat, black bob finished off her stylish look perfectly. She wouldn't have looked out of place on a poster advertising some high-end designer boutique. 'Swankier than our usual chicken and chips, but I got a good bonus this year, so order what you want – it's on me.'

◆———— • ● ◆ ● • ———— ◆

A bottle and a half of Sauvignon Blanc later, it was just like old times. Katie was chatting away at what felt like a million words a minute, waving her glass emphatically, and Gloria laughed along to her latest stories and escapades. It was a breath of fresh air after weeks cooped up at home, and as their conversation continued, Gloria began to realise how much she'd missed her friend.

'Anyway, enough about me,' Katie said, wiping a tear of laughter from her eye following her latest tale from the corporate world. 'We're here for you! I've been a busy bee, and I stumbled on an opportunity for you, Gloria, that I think you'll be very excited about!'

Butterflies fluttered in Gloria's stomach. She had got so used to her slow-paced, quiet lifestyle, she actually felt a little nervous at the prospect of something new. *I'm not an adventurer any more*, she thought with a surprising pang of sadness. It had been her decision to settle down back in the UK, after all.

'When I was last in London,' Katie's eyes sparkled with excitement as she continued, oblivious to Gloria's unease, 'I was working a corporate networking event. You know, schmoosing potential clients, that sort of thing. Anyway, I met a very interesting person – Meryl Hofmann-Mills, have you heard of her?'

The name was familiar. It conjured up a memory from a long time ago that was just outside her grasp, like when a recognisable smell stirred a feeling within her she just couldn't place.

'I think so, but you're going to have to refresh my memory...'

Katie rolled her eyes in an exaggerated manner. 'Typical Glor, head in the clouds!' She smiled and gave Gloria a little wink to make it obvious she was joking. 'She's an art dealer, mostly holding shows around Europe, but she's got a gallery in London now, and I think your paintings would be just perfect for it. She's offered to look at your work and consider it for her next exhibition! Isn't that exciting?'

Gloria was shell-shocked, and it took her a moment or two to realise her mouth was hanging open. She now knew why the name rang a bell – there was a Hofmann-Mills show in Amsterdam every year! She'd gone herself one summer and marvelled at the array of exquisite pieces on display. She'd even used a few of them for inspiration for some more risqué pieces she'd experimented with in her younger days, although she'd never admit that now. Yes, she was proud of some of her paintings, but *her* work on display at a Hofmann-Mills gallery? The very idea was incredible.

'Well?' Katie prodded, waving a hand in front of Gloria's face. 'Are you going to gawp at me all afternoon or are you going to give me an answer?'

'Well, that's, um, exciting!' Gloria managed to blurt out, her head spinning. 'But I haven't sold a painting for months, and even then it's usually just to small-time venues and cafés. How could she want to feature *my* work?'

'I've shown her your paintings, babe.' Katie grinned, topping up their wine glasses. 'Oh, no need to look so violated! After I spoke to her, I had a rummage through my old hard drives and found some photos we'd taken when we were trying to push your work back in 'Dam.'

She continued pouring out the wine in silence, and the

seconds seemed to drag on for eternity as Gloria waited to hear what Meryl Hofmann-Mills had thought of the – of *her* – paintings. She couldn't believe Katie had gone ahead and shown them to her without asking first. Her insides squirmed.

'She loved them, Glor! And when I told her you'd improved since those days, she was very keen to see more. This is it, girl. You did it!'

Katie giggled as Gloria's hands shot up to her mouth in excitement, sending her full glass flying across the table and soaking them both in what she was sure was very expensive white wine.

Katie grinned, getting the table back in some semblance of order and shaking her head at her friend. 'Shall I set up a meeting, then?'

Gloria's stomach tightened as she considered meeting face to face with Meryl Hofmann-Mills. She had admired her work for years while they were in Amsterdam, and the idea of her paintings being displayed beside them was thrilling and terrifying at the same time. It was all a little overwhelming. She wondered what Greg would say.

'I don't suppose I could have a day or two to think it over?'

'Talk it over with Greg, you mean?' Katie raised her eyebrows and took Gloria's hand across the table, her eyes softening. 'It's *your* life, Glor. You can make your own decisions. This is such an exciting opportunity for you, and it's just *one* meeting. Why not?'

Maybe it was the alcohol coursing through her veins, or the intoxication of being reunited with her old friend, but Gloria was blurting out the words before she could stop herself.

'Yes. I'll do it!'

The rest of the day passed in a blissful, tipsy blur. Katie revealed she had booked the day off work, and she and Gloria spent the afternoon strolling around the city, heading nowhere in particular. As they sat on the South Bank, drinking cold cider outside a small, quirky bar, it felt just like old times. The River Thames shone in the late afternoon sun, and it was like they were back in Amsterdam, just two carefree twenty-year-olds with no plan for tomorrow, just living for today.

'What are you smiling at?' Katie asked, taking a drag from her cigarette.

'It's just...nice, isn't it? Like back in the old days. Having a cheeky drink before a night at the club. The only thing missing is Hendrick hovering around.'

Katie let out a loud laugh at that, attracting the attention of the people at the nearest table, but she didn't seem to notice.

'I'd almost forgotten about him! Good old Hendrick. He was a dear, though, wasn't he? We were lucky he was there to get us out of a few scrapes!'

'Lucky he fancied you more like!' Gloria laughed, and the two of them burst into a fit of giggles. 'God, who would have thought we'd end up where we are now?'

'Hey, at least you're living the dream, unlike me.' Katie barked a laugh. 'Lovely husband, beautiful house, gorgeous daughter...I guess we always knew I'd be the corporate sellout,' she added, putting her cigarette out in the overflowing ashtray in the middle of the table.

Something Katie had said alerted Gloria's attention. *Beautiful house, gorgeous daughter...*

Shit! She'd forgotten to call Iris!

◆——— • ● ◆ ● • ——— ◆

'I know, I know, I'm late.' *Again.* 'I'm so sorry.'

'Do you know what time it is over here?' Iris's voice was filled with disapproval. 'And what's all that noise?'

'There's only an hour's difference. You remember I used to live there, right?' Gloria smiled at the camera, hoping her light-heartedness would be picked up through the video call and brighten up her very impatient daughter's mood. Teenagers were so sensitive; she had to remind herself of that fact every time they spoke, it seemed. 'And I'm on the train back from London.'

At that, Iris's mood did seem to improve somewhat. 'What, you're actually out doing something?' Iris giggled, raising her eyebrows at her mother. 'King Greg let you out of the castle for a day?'

Gloria laughed. Greg and Iris got along well enough, but he was from a very different world to the one Iris had grown up in, and because of that, he was often teased about his privileged upbringing.

'Hey, you've got a very cool, active mum, thank you very much.' Gloria couldn't say it with a straight face; they both knew she was practically a hermit nowadays. This was confirmed as Iris snorted with laughter in reply.

'Maybe, a long time ago, when you were my age.' Her

forehead creased into a slight frown. 'Before you met Greg.'

'Now, come on, that's not fair. Greg doesn't make me stay at home, you know that. I've just grown up, that's all. I've got to get all my painting done before I turn into an old woman. I am turning forty soon, after all!'

That comment seemed to cheer Iris up, and she was soon chatting away as she lost herself in planning a lavish birthday party for her mother, complete with a champagne fountain and an array of A-list VIP guests. Iris might be sixteen soon, but she was still a mummy's girl at heart.

'You'll come back to Amsterdam for it, right, Mum?' Iris chattered excitedly, glittering blue eyes gleaming at the prospect of a reunion.

Gloria hesitated, her chest tightening. 'Well, that depends, sweetheart...'

'On Greg?' Iris fixed her mother with a cold stare. No, it was more than cold – she was hurt.

'No, um, that's not what I meant. But you know how tricky trips are to arrange, and—'

'That's fine. I get it.'

A few awkward moments of silence passed. Gloria was about to attempt to break the tension when Iris got in first.

'Look, I'd better go. Dad will be home soon, and I'm sure you're nearly at your station. Just...think about your birthday, yeah? We miss you.'

Gloria didn't know what to say, but luckily her phone beeped to tell her Iris had hung up. It seemed she wasn't going to wait for a response. *Or she didn't want to get one and be disappointed*, Gloria thought with a sigh. She had tried so hard to maintain the closeness they shared before she left for the UK, but it felt like Iris was slipping away from her.

GLORIA

She closed her eyes and rested her head against the glass of the carriage window as the train trundled onwards towards home, feeling deflated.

◆——— • ● ◆ ● • ———◆

By the time the taxi pulled up at the bottom of the long driveway, Gloria's spirits had lifted somewhat. She'd had time to relive her conversation with Katie about the potential gallery deal, and was giddy with excitement all over again. She practically floated through the door into the spacious, high-ceilinged hallway and on into the kitchen, throwing her jacket down on one of the stools around the breakfast bar.

Pouring herself a celebratory glass of Merlot, Gloria set off through the house in search of Greg. It was a shame they didn't have any champagne, or at least Prosecco, to celebrate properly and toast her good news with a glass of bubbly. She'd have to remember to get some tomorrow. Skipping upstairs, Gloria felt lighter and freer than she had for an awfully long time, and she giggled as the wine started to go to her head.

Wandering through the first floor of the vast house, Gloria was disappointed to discover Greg was working in his study. The door was closed, but she could hear him speaking on the phone to some client or other. Gloria wasn't strictly banned from the room, but Greg had made it perfectly clear that his work contained highly confidential medical records, and it could compromise his career if Gloria were to accidentally stumble upon some information she wasn't supposed to see. It didn't matter; she would tell Greg her news tomorrow.

CHAPTER THREE

Gloria smiled as she slid the bottle into the fridge, her chest fluttering. She was quite proud of her choice of champagne, having made the effort to do some advance research into which one would perfectly match the salmon she'd bought for dinner. This was a special occasion, after all.

As she fussed around the kitchen, checking temperatures and stirring pans, she glanced impatiently at the large silver clock gleaming against the black slate tiles. Greg would be home any minute, but she was so excited to tell him all about the gallery, she didn't want to wait another second. She couldn't remember the last time she had felt this exhilarated and wanted nothing more than to share it with her husband. Turning everything down to a low simmer, she dashed upstairs to check her hair and makeup again.

Gloria was tracing a soft pink lipstick across her bottom lip when she finally heard Greg's Mercedes roll up the driveway. She was usually too absorbed in her painting to notice him arriving home, but her senses felt heightened this evening. She jumped up from her dressing table and took a second to admire her reflection in the mirror. With a twinge of sadness, she realised it had been a long time since she'd made herself up like this, but she shook it off and scurried downstairs to greet her husband.

'Something smells good.' Greg grinned as he sauntered into the kitchen, suit jacket casually slung over his shoulder. 'No egg and chips today?'

'Oh, ha ha,' Gloria retorted. It was no secret that Gloria's culinary prowess left much to be desired, but she could whip up something special when she needed to. 'I thought I'd treat us both today, so we have line-caught salmon baked in rosemary and thyme, with a creamy garlic sauce and fresh veggies.'

Greg raised an eyebrow, impressed. 'Very good! What's the occasion?'

'No occasion,' Gloria teased with a small smile. 'But I may have some interesting news!'

Greg's eyes widened with a look of genuine intrigue. 'Well, let's not waste any time then, get dinner dished up and spill the beans!'

As the pair settled down at the dinner table, Gloria inwardly congratulated herself for using the good dinnerware and setting the table so attractively. Unlike the neighbours and the few of Greg's well-to-do colleagues that Gloria had dined with in recent years, she hadn't learned any kind of etiquette growing up, and it had taken time to master laying everything out perfectly.

'So,' Greg began, leaning back in his chair and taking a swig of wine from the crystal glasses Gloria had retrieved from the back of the kitchen cabinet. 'What's inspired all this then?'

'Well, you know I had lunch with Katie yesterday in the city?' At this, Greg rolled his eyes; he'd made his opinions about Katie perfectly clear the other day, but Gloria ignored him and continued. 'Well, she's made a connection with a professional art dealer, Meryl Hofmann-Mills. Have you heard of her?'

Unsurprisingly, Greg simply shrugged. He'd never taken an interest in the world of the arts; he was a scientist and a businessman through and through.

'Well,' Gloria continued excitedly, 'Katie showed her some of my work, and it seems she actually likes it and might want some pieces for her gallery! She's going to pop by and have a look at my latest paintings on Monday. Isn't that wonderful?'

Greg smiled and reached across the table to take Gloria's hands in his. Where Gloria's eyes glittered with excitement, Greg's face offered something very different. Gloria thought it almost looked like pity. Her stomach tightened in anticipation.

'Oh, my beautiful, naive wife,' he began, stroking the back of Gloria's hand with his thumb. 'I'm sure Katie meant well, but it was a little unkind of her to let you show your pictures to a professional.'

Gloria was stunned. For a second, she simply blinked and stared back at her husband, her brain trying to make sense of his words.

'What...what do you mean? Katie said Meryl loved the photos she showed her.'

'Well, she would say that, wouldn't she?' Greg chuckled, shaking his head at his wife. 'She's trying to give you confidence. But, really, she's just setting you up for a bigger fall in the end, which wasn't very fair.'

Gloria felt like she'd been punched in the stomach. Would Katie really lie to her like that? She had seemed so genuine when they had talked together, but perhaps she was just humouring her old friend. Gloria's mouth was suddenly very dry, and she couldn't get any words out. She took a swig of wine from her glass to settle her shaking hands.

'So, you don't think I should meet with her?' she managed to squeak. 'The dealer?'

Greg placed a comforting hand on Gloria's arm. 'I won't tell you what to do, darling. This is *your* hobby. If you don't mind the risk of embarrassment and want to give it a shot, then I'll support you. I just hope you don't hit the bottle too hard when the inevitable rejection comes.'

With that, he scraped up the last piece of salmon into his mouth and stood up to leave. 'I have to call a client. I won't be long. Fabulous meal, darling.'

He kissed the top of Gloria's head and left her sat at the table, frozen in place like a statue. After a few dazed moments, she buckled as a wave of emotion wracked her body. Her wine glass, forgotten and dangling loosely from her fingers, crashed across the table as she buried her head in her hands.

She felt so *embarrassed*.

Rising from the table, Gloria collected their plates with trembling hands and made her way into the kitchen. She shuffled across the gleaming, white marble floor, her feet feeling as if they were made of lead. Dumping the plates into the sink, she glanced at the fridge at the end of the counter and grimaced, remembering the bottle of champagne left unopened within. She wouldn't be able to bring herself to tell Greg she'd bought it. He'd think she was stupid. Well, she was, wasn't she? She'd actually believed that she could show her amateur paintings to a world-renowned art dealer without making a fool of herself.

Gloria's eyes brimmed with hot tears as she took out her

mobile phone and searched for Katie's number. Feeling too ashamed to call her friend, she typed a brief message with unsteady fingers.

> Sorry, I can't do it, I have to cancel. Please apologise to Meryl for me.

Her stomach clenched as she pressed "send". She should have known it was too good to be true.

CHAPTER FOUR

Gloria spent the weekend in a daze of grim solemnity, drifting through the house like a ghost haunting her own home. She felt drained, hollow.

Greg didn't seem to notice; he spent Saturday golfing with some clients and Sunday saw him holed up in his study for much of the day. As long as his dinner was on the table at the end of the day, he was satisfied. Gloria was used to it: the long days of solitude, the loneliness of the cold, empty bed when he didn't return to it until sleep had already taken her. It was sometimes difficult, but this time she felt a deep sense of relief to not have to face him after the embarrassment of the other night.

By the time Monday came around, Gloria felt almost normal again, and forced herself to return to her garden studio and confront her mediocrity head-on. In truth, she hadn't started painting to gain success. Art was her outlet, a primal need that allowed her to feel free, at peace and, frankly, herself. However, she'd be lying if she said there hadn't always been a glimmer of hope in the back of her mind that one of her pieces would make it somewhere special one day. Not for fame or fortune, but for the sheer pride of getting her work out there, and knowing that people, if only a handful of art fans, were getting enjoyment out of it.

With a heavy sigh, she turned the key to the door of her studio and stepped inside. It was another gorgeous summer day, and the late morning sun glowed through the large windows, illuminating Gloria's haphazardly scattered brushes and palettes and giving them a surreal shimmer. Her short break away from the studio had entrapped a strong odour of paint and solvents which hadn't had the chance to ventilate, but rather than open the windows to relieve herself of the scent, Gloria breathed it in deeply. People might see her art as a hobby, but she didn't care. Here, in this studio, she was home, and no one could take that away from her.

She shook her head, forcing down the irritation that was bubbling up inside of her. She shouldn't be angry at Greg. After all, it was his support that allowed her to spend so much time painting in the first place. He was the one who had stopped her from applying for jobs to focus on her art, on top of providing support payments for Iris on her behalf. A knot of guilt slowly formed in her stomach; she really had been taking Greg for granted lately. She would have to make it up to him.

Taking one last comforting inhale of the aromas of her work, Gloria threw open two of the long windows and started to set up for her next piece. Without thinking, her hands reached out to the tubes of blues and greens she kept by her easel at all times. The colours of the sea.

◆———— • ● ◆ ● • ————◆

The hours slipped by quickly when Gloria was lost in her work, and she had lost all sense of time when the loud chime of the doorbell shook her out of her dream-like state. She glanced down at her phone, realising she'd completely forgotten to have lunch and it was already past three o'clock. Shoving her brushes into the pocket of her dungarees, she smoothed her hair away from her face and wandered through the house to the front door.

As she searched for her keys, Gloria absent-mindedly wondered who might be at the door. Despite Gloria being home most days, Greg usually got any packages delivered directly to his office. She would often go all day without being disturbed. Finally locating her keys by a discarded wine glass on the coffee table in the lounge, she returned to the door and swung it open.

'Gloria Harrison, I presume?'

It took a long moment for Gloria to respond, as she stood gaping at the visitor with her mouth open. A week ago, Gloria probably wouldn't have recognised the short, well-dressed middle-aged woman standing before her, but her considerable research following her lunch date with Katie left her in no doubt whatsoever that this was Meryl Hofmann-Mills.

'I-I'm sorry,' Gloria stammered, almost lost for words. 'I thought Katie had cancelled our meeting today?'

'She certainly tried to.' Meryl chuckled. Her voice was pleasant, almost musical, enveloping Gloria and putting her at ease. Her smile was one of warm affability. 'But I'm not one to back down that easily, especially because of a case of nerves. May I come in?'

Gloria blinked and stepped aside as Meryl swept into the hallway. Despite being such a small figure, her personality seemed to fill the entire room. She paused and surveyed the large, open space, her messy bun of white-gold hair bobbing as her head swivelled left and right.

'What a beautiful home. A little stark for my taste, but still, lovely. Now,' she added, turning back to face Gloria with a wide smile, her kind brown eyes twinkling. 'Let's see this studio of yours.'

Gloria tried to hide the tremble in her hands as she held open the door for Meryl Hofmann-Mills to enter her studio. Although the woman had been extremely polite so far, Gloria was bracing herself for the no doubt scathing critique which would spill from her once she laid eyes on her paintings. At the back of her mind, she couldn't help but curse Katie for springing this on her when she had asked her to cancel. Had she really told Meryl that she'd backed out because of a case of nerves? The cheek!

Gloria snapped back to attention when she noticed Meryl examining her latest work-in-progress on the easel, still glistening with fresh paint.

'Oh, don't look at that! Erm, sorry...' she stuttered as Meryl raised a confused eyebrow in response to her startled cry. 'It's just, this is a piece I started today to help me relax. It wasn't what I wanted to show you.'

Meryl turned back to the painting and studied it for several agonisingly long moments. Gloria was acutely aware of the volume of her rapid breathing and tried to settle herself.

'Well, it's clear it's unfinished,' Meryl stated, and Gloria felt her insides tighten. Here it was, the tear-down. She hadn't even had a chance to show Meryl her best pieces.

Damn it, Katie, why are you putting me through this?

'But I like it. There's a great deal of passion here, and such interesting combinations of colour. Let's see what else you've got.'

◆———— • ● ◆ ● • ———— ◆

Gloria grinned from ear to ear as she waved Meryl off from her doorway. The older woman returned her smile from the front seat of her vintage yellow Triumph convertible as she started down the long driveway to the main road. Despite her initial anxiety, Gloria had thoroughly enjoyed her afternoon with Meryl. The art dealer's easy-going, gracious manner had put Gloria at ease incredibly quickly, and they had soon found themselves laughing together about the nonsensicality of the European art scene of the nineties over glasses of red wine.

Despite her fame and fortune, Meryl was surprisingly down to Earth and thoroughly pleasant company. Gloria had relaxed in a way she was now realising she hadn't done for years. Once she had forgotten that Meryl was here to judge her work, Gloria had revelled in having a fellow art enthusiast around again, and her nerves had given way to a confidence and social energy she had forgotten she possessed.

It had obviously paid off, too. As Gloria closed the door, she couldn't help but smile down at the monochrome business card Meryl had placed in her hand before leaving.

'Stop doubting yourself.' She had smiled as she folded Gloria's fingers over the card. 'You've got talent, and you should give yourself a chance. Call me.'

Goosebumps prickled Gloria's skin as she turned the card over and over between her forefingers and thumbs. She brushed a thumb over the delicately embossed lettering, a rush of emotion flooding her body. She could not quite pinpoint what she was feeling. Excitement, of course, but something else slowly bubbled up to the surface. Fear.

While in Meryl's company, she was confident, relaxed, self-assured. Now, as the intoxication of the visit began to wear off, those wonderful feelings threatened to harden to cold lead in the pit of Gloria's stomach.

She shook her head, willing the creeping anxiety away and focusing on the glimmer of success she had glimpsed this afternoon. She wandered over to the coat stand by the door, clutching the card carefully as if handling something fragile. A cautious smile slowly spread across her face as she stowed it safely in a handbag hanging snugly between Greg's various blazers and coats.

Gloria was chopping carrots in the kitchen when she heard Greg's car pull up outside. Her head was still spinning from her afternoon with Meryl, but she ignored the quivering in her stomach to focus on preparing dinner. She might have complete freedom during the day, but Greg was quite insistent on Gloria putting dinner on the table every evening. Although cooking was not at the top of her list of favourite things to do, she didn't complain. After all, Greg had not only rescued Gloria from her unstable life overseas, he had made sure Iris grew up in a safe, secure environment as well. She owed him everything.

'Honey, I'm home!' Greg called from the hallway, and Gloria felt herself jump a little at the sudden sound of his voice.

'In here!' she answered, resuming her chopping as Greg strolled into the kitchen and dropped his laptop case on the nearest stool. He was impeccably dressed, as always. Leaning on the kitchen counter, he looked like he'd walked straight out of a catalogue.

'What, you couldn't wait for me?' he laughed, and Gloria turned to face him, confused. He nodded towards the two empty wine glasses abandoned on the counter after Meryl had left.

'Oh...sorry,' Gloria's cheeks reddened, and she hoped Greg didn't notice. 'You know what I'm like when I'm cooking. Refill?'

CHAPTER FIVE

The next few days were a whirlwind of artistic endeavour, as Gloria's creativity thrummed with a renewed energy she hadn't experienced in years. She spent more time than ever in the studio, creating vivid landscapes awash with colour and vibrancy. No longer was she painting as a means of escape. She felt like she had a real purpose again, a goal to work towards and a spark of self-belief she hadn't even noticed she'd lost until now. It was like she was coming alive again, her anxieties melting away in a flurry of brushstrokes.

When she wasn't in front of a canvas, Gloria found herself drawn once more to the balcony. Perhaps it was her recent reconnection with Katie, or maybe it was meeting Meryl Hofmann-Mills. She wasn't sure, but either way, she couldn't stop her mind from returning to her past life overseas.

No matter where she had travelled, even in the most densely packed cities, she had always had the water by her side. Crowds of people had surrounded her, but by the water, she felt free and at peace. It didn't matter that she didn't know how she would pay for next week's rent, or where her next train ticket would come from; she was calm. Now, the river was something she could only hope to see on a clear day when the clouds parted enough for her to watch her dreams of new adventures wash away with the current.

In the cool evenings, there was a brisk wind ripping through the trees, and even from this distance, Gloria could see the river's waters churn and roil like molten metal in the darkness, shining in the moonlight. Standing at her bedroom window, Gloria felt as though she could step out onto its surface and glide over the steely currents as if walking on a frozen lake, knowing it could somehow hold her weight. Sometimes, on her darker days, she had wished it wouldn't, and she would be engulfed by the torrents and lost.

♦———— • • ♦ • • ———— ♦

'I'm sorry, the person you are calling is unavailable.
To leave a message–'

Gloria hung up and looked at her phone in confusion. It wasn't like Iris to miss their weekly phone calls; if anything, Gloria was the one who was usually late or was pulled away by Greg to attend some function or dinner. When Iris didn't answer yesterday, she had decided to give her some space and try again. But she had called twice more to no response. She knew Iris was growing up and might have other priorities right now, but she had always been a well-behaved girl, and Gloria was starting to get a little worried. She would have to call Elias.

Elias picked up after a few rings. 'Hello, Gloria.' He seemed uncharacteristically abrupt, and Gloria was taken aback. Yes, he was an ex, but they'd remained good friends since the break-up. She even found herself missing him sometimes, when she was alone.

'Elias? Are you okay? Is Iris okay?' She took a breath to slow herself down. 'It's just...she missed our call and hasn't been picking up, so—'

'I'm fine.' Again, he sounded off. Cold, even. 'Iris is safe, if that's what you mean, but I've got to tell you, Gloria, she's pretty crushed about this whole birthday thing. Especially having to hear it second hand from Greg. God, Gloria, couldn't you have at least broken the news to her yourself?'

'What...what do you mean?' Gloria was confused. Yes, Iris hadn't been happy that she hadn't committed to travelling back to Amsterdam for her birthday, but what did Greg have to do with it?

'I'm not getting into an argument about it over the phone,' Elias replied. 'Look, I know we're not together anymore, and it's none of my business if you want to swan off with Greg to some luxury resort for your big birthday. You do you. But Iris is my daughter too, and when you let her down, I'm the one who has to pick up the pieces over here.'

Gloria didn't know what to say. This conversation wasn't making any sense.

'Elias, I don't know what Greg has said to you, or to Iris. I don't know what you're talking about!'

'Please give me some credit, Glor.' Elias huffed, and Gloria could almost hear his eyes rolling at the other side of the phone. 'You barely speak to Iris these days as it is, and now you're getting Greg to let her down so you don't have to be the bad guy.'

'That's not it at all!'

'Just...give her a couple of days, okay?' Elias's tone softened a little, and Gloria was relieved to hear some of its usual warmth return. 'She's really stressed with school right now, and I think the thought of seeing you for your birthday was giving her something to look forward to. I've got to go, I'm at work, but call her again in a few days. I'm sure she'll be fine.'

The phone beeped as the connection was lost, leaving Gloria sat frozen on the sofa staring at the empty space in front of her. She was dumbfounded. Why had Greg spoken to Iris about her birthday? They had barely spoken about it to each other, and she hadn't even broached the idea of going to Amsterdam with him yet.

She would have to confront him.

When Greg's Mercedes finally rolled up the driveway, Gloria braced herself behind the breakfast bar and took a large mouthful of red wine from the glass in her hand. As usual, he wandered into the kitchen, looking pleased with himself after no doubt another successful day at work, but his face dropped somewhat when he looked over at Gloria. She'd had time to work herself into a mild rage whilst waiting for her husband to come home, and it must have shown on her face.

'Has something happened, babe?' Greg asked slowly, his forehead creasing in apparent concern.

'Why did you call Iris about my birthday?'

There, she'd said it.

Greg smiled, and his lapsed confidence started to creep back into his face. 'I see someone's blown the surprise.' He threw up his hands in mock exasperation. 'Trust a teenager to not be able to keep a secret.'

'Don't go blaming Iris. She's so devastated she won't even talk to me!' Gloria felt her voice rise, and wine splashed over the side of her glass as she slammed a hand down on the counter.

'If not Iris, then who?' Greg asked quietly, raising an eyebrow.

Oops.

'Elias,' Gloria said, allowing her voice to soften a little. 'I had to call him to check she was okay. She's been dodging my calls for days because of what you said to her.'

'I thought you barely spoke to him nowadays?' Greg stepped closer to the breakfast bar, eyes fixed on Gloria. 'Iris misses a couple of calls from you and you're straight on the phone to your ex-boyfriend?'

'What are you trying to say?' Gloria asked, incredulous. 'He's Iris's dad. I had to check she was okay.'

'She's fifteen, for God's sake.' Greg had his hands on the breakfast bar, his face now level with Gloria's, eyes boring into hers. 'But she knows what she's doing, I'll give her that.'

She was taken aback. 'What do you mean?'

'I call up to give her the news I'm whisking my lovely wife off on a once-in-a-lifetime mini-cruise for her big birthday, and she uses it as an excuse to bring you and Daddy closer together.' He huffed and rolled his eyes.

Gloria hesitated. *No, that can't be right.*

'Elias said she was crushed. She was hoping we'd both go over to Amsterdam.'

'Hoping *you* would go over.' He forced out a small laugh, shaking his head. 'Open your eyes, Gloria! She's taking the piss. She knows I struggle to get time off, so was planting a seed to get you over there while I'm working.'

'Well, I don't know about that...'

'It hurts, you know.' Greg's eyes glistened, now just inches away from Gloria's own. Piercing brown against startled blue. 'We don't get to spend much time together, and I know it's because I'm working, I know. But I'm working for *us*. For me, for you *and* for Iris. Lord knows, her dad couldn't put her through International School. I manage to book a trip for the two of us and try to be romantic for a fucking change, and yet I'm the bad guy?'

He turned away, running a hand through his hair. Gloria reached over and tried to put her hand on his shoulder, but he shrugged it off. A shiver of guilt ran through her, pushing out the last remnants of her anger.

'Look,' she walked around the breakfast bar to face him, but he looked straight down at the floor, crestfallen. 'Booking a trip was a wonderful idea, and I'm grateful, I really am. It's just hearing about Iris being upset really got to me. I should've asked for your side before I got angry. I'm sorry.'

A long moment passed, and Greg lifted his head. Relief washed over Gloria as she saw he was smiling again.

CHAPTER SIX

Following their altercation about Iris, Gloria felt obliged to accept when Greg invited her to his company's garden party the following weekend. It was some corporate affair, where Greg would no doubt be off sweet-talking clients for much of the day whilst Gloria engaged in awkward small talk with his colleagues. She knew she would hate it, but what choice did she have? She was Greg's wife; it was expected of her. His only instruction had been to "look her best", and he'd even bought her a new cocktail dress for the occasion.

'Perfect to make those sapphire eyes pop,' he had said with a wink as he handed the bag over to her.

Gloria turned in her seat at the dresser and glanced over at the dress hanging on the wardrobe. It was a chic, knee-length, navy blue number and, although it was a bit more glamorous than her usual style, she had to admit it was beautiful, and undoubtedly very expensive. She had known from their first meeting that Greg liked the finer things in life, but Gloria wasn't interested in flashy cars or designer clothes. She just wanted safety and security, for both herself and for Iris. Ever since she'd first seen that blurry shape on the ultrasound screen, she had promised her unborn baby that they would have a better start in life than she had.

And I will keep that promise.

A pang of sadness struck Gloria as she remembered how things were between Iris and her at the moment. She hoped Greg was right, that Iris was exaggerating how upset she was about missing her mother's birthday, but the idea of her own daughter trying to manipulate her like that made Gloria feel even worse. This certainly wasn't how she had planned for parenthood to be, but Iris was getting the best possible opportunities this way. One day she would see that and understand.

'Don't tell me you're still in your robe!' Greg's sudden voice knocked Gloria out of her daze, and she turned to see him leaning in the bedroom doorway, a mischievous grin plastered across his face. 'Come on, darling, if I'm going to show you off to my new clients, I need you to be ready in plenty of time.'

He lingered for a moment longer, and then was gone. It was easy enough for Greg – he looked charming and sophisticated every day. It was second nature to him. Gloria rarely did more than scoop her red curls up into a loose ponytail and throw on some dungarees to protect herself from stray splashes of paint. However, she had promised Greg she would make an effort, so she dug out her makeup bag and an old can of hairspray, and managed to make herself look reasonably presentable.

'Ta-da!' she announced as she unsteadily navigated the wide staircase in her rarely used black high heels. 'How do I look?'

Greg was waiting by the door, dressed immaculately in a perfectly tailored pale grey suit. He smiled up at his wife, his brown eyes glittering. 'Absolutely perfect. Let's go.'

◆———— • ● ◆ ● • ————◆

Despite Greg's positive reassurances about her appearance, Gloria was wracked with nerves as she stepped out of the Mercedes onto the forecourt of the imposing manor house where the party was to be held. She had been to a handful of Greg's company functions before, but they'd never been this...*grand.* Her breath caught as she took in the magnificent white-stone facade, looking out over the River Wey. Perfectly ordered rows of tall rectangular windows reflected its sparkling, slow-moving waters.

As they approached, Gloria was vaguely aware of Greg saying something about the manor house being renovated and transformed into a high-end hotel, but it didn't sink in, unable to penetrate the shroud of anxiety building up around her. The vast building seemed to loom over them as they passed into its shadow, and Gloria could not shake the feeling that it somehow knew she did not belong here. She was an imposter.

Greg linked his arm through hers, and she struggled to keep up with him as he strolled confidently around the side of the house to the lush gardens beyond. She could not hold back an audible gasp as she took in the sheer scale of the event. The grounds of the house were substantial, seemingly stretching all the way to the horizon, where a faint line of trees was vaguely visible against the clear, blue summer sky. The stretch of land bordering the house was made up of perfectly manicured lawns encircled by breathtaking floral displays, each so flawless they could have come straight from the Chelsea Flower Show. What shocked Gloria, however, was the number of people. There must have been two hundred bodies milling around the gardens, men and women alike looking like they had materialised from the pages of a fashion magazine. She had never felt more intimidated.

'You didn't say there would be so many people,' she whispered to Greg, who didn't seem to hear.

He simply continued walking forward, ignoring the more discreet paths around the edge of the lawns and instead pulling Gloria directly down one running through the centre of the party. She could feel heat flooding to her face as a great many pairs of eyes focused on them. She became painfully aware of how uncomfortable her shoes were and, even more worrying, how unsteady she felt walking in them. Her heartbeat quickened in her chest as a hot ball of anxiety turned in her stomach.

'I told you I wanted to show you off,' Greg answered finally, as they neared the end of the path. He tugged on her arm and steered her off to the left, towards a small group of women gathered around a tall, white table, each holding a glass of wine in their hand. Gloria's skin prickled as she realised they had already noticed her approach, their eyes fixed on hers, small smiles on their faces.

'Ladies!' Greg greeted them enthusiastically, kissing each one on the cheek. 'Victoria, Lucy, Nina – you remember Gloria, right?'

Gloria didn't recognise any of the three women stood before her, but she greeted them all with a, 'So nice to see you again,' and, unsure of how to conduct herself in this sort of situation, an awkward handshake. They replied with the appropriate level of civility for the occasion, but Gloria was sure she saw Victoria – a tall, leggy blonde with an aura of the alpha female about her – look her up and down before nodding to Greg as if in approval.

A little work-related small-talk followed, with Gloria dutifully nodding along to the conversation between the four colleagues, not understanding a word they were saying. Greg didn't talk about work much at home since the medical jargon went straight over her head, but from what she understood, his company, Genisolve, manipulated DNA for the betterment of humanity. That's how he had phrased it, anyway. He was clearly passionate about his work – he often put in extra hours at home or in the office, going above and beyond to please his demanding clients – but it was a world Gloria rarely intruded upon, and they were both content with that arrangement.

Despite the technical nature of the company, Gloria never failed to be surprised by how corporate their functions seemed to be. There was always a sheen of glamour about the place, with buzzwords liberally thrown about like a press release for the latest must-have device. Each conversation was laced with shallow flattery, and Gloria doubted whether any of the overenthusiastic compliments were genuine. She couldn't stand it, but put on her best "that's so interesting" face regardless.

'Now,' Greg suddenly turned to Gloria, who until then had been a spectator to his conversation. 'I need to mingle. These clients won't schmooze themselves!'

Gloria's stomach tightened. Surely he wasn't going to leave her to navigate the party by herself already? She tried to catch Greg's eye, to implore him not to leave her, but he paid little heed to her silent, wide-eyed plea.

'Can I rely on you lovely ladies to look after Gloria for a while?'

Oh no.

She may have been able to handle being left alone to awkwardly accept drinks and canapés from the waiting staff, but the very idea of a prolonged time trying not to embarrass herself in front these three people sent her head spinning.

'Don't you want me to join you?' she asked, trying to keep her voice light. She was almost sure she heard a quiet laugh come from Victoria, but when she glanced to her left, the woman's face was as amicable as ever.

'Don't worry,' Nina said, stepping between Gloria and Greg with a devilish smile, blocking any means of following. 'We don't bite.'

CHAPTER SEVEN

Gloria managed to slip away to the drinks table after thirty excruciating minutes of interrogation. The three women seemed to have an endless supply of questions, and Gloria couldn't help but wonder if they'd chosen the ones they were sure would make her squirm the most. They'd asked what university she'd gone to (none), where she'd grown up (Yorkshire), even what her parents did for a living (Gloria had managed to make something up on the spot for that one).

Why were these people so insistent on mining her for information? She could only assume they meant to make her feel inferior around all of these highly educated, middle-class people. And it worked – it was humiliating.

Gloria held back tears as she approached the drinks table and threw back two glasses of Prosecco. How long would it take for her to feel like an equal amongst Greg's friends and colleagues? Would they ever see her as anything but a working-class idiot who Greg had taken pity on and brought down to leafy, comfortable Surrey to look after like some kind of charity case? Gloria always worked so hard to be good enough for Greg, and yet, in this moment, it felt like it would never be enough.

She let out a heavy sigh. Here she was, surrounded by people yet feeling lonelier than ever. All around her, sophisticated executives chatted and laughed, but she could never be a part of it. She wasn't one of them. Taking a deep breath, she picked up another full glass and headed back towards the garden where Lucy, Nina and Victoria were no doubt waiting to continue their tear-down. She felt like a mouse being batted around by three sleek Persian cats, toying with her for their amusement. Gloria had made it almost halfway back to the group when she noticed the sign for the ladies' toilets. Without thinking about it, she broke away from the path and made a beeline for the sanctuary they offered.

As luck would have it, the room was empty when Gloria entered, so she dove into the nearest cubicle, hoping to compose herself before heading back out into the fray. Sitting down on the toilet lid, she raked a hand through her crimson curls and let out a heavy sigh. When had she become this pathetic person? She thought back to her twenties, comfortable in any situation, sometimes even the life and soul of the party. She'd been poor and work was usually unstable, but her unbridled optimism and passion had always pulled her through. Now, she had everything she could ever need, and yet she felt like a frightened teenager again, being picked apart by the popular girls at school.

'—best ever, if you ask me. They're going down a treat with the clients.'

The door swung open and closed as someone entered the room. The sudden interruption snapped Gloria's attention back to the present. She sat frozen in the cubicle, hoping whoever it was wouldn't be here for long. She did not want to be discovered hiding in the toilets.

'Did you see Greg's wife?' a second voice joined the conversation, and Gloria's chest tightened. She couldn't be sure, but it sounded an awful lot like Victoria.

'I'm not sure, which one is she?'

'Red hair, blue eyes, a bit scruffy.'

'Oh, the one in the blue dress? I *thought* she looked like a deer caught in headlights!' The other woman let out a sharp laugh. 'The clients were all watching her, no doubt.'

'Yes. I think Greg's done well with her. We'll just have to make sure she's seen and not heard. Have you heard her accent? Atrocious!'

The two women giggled, unaware that the focus of their conversation was mere feet away from them, sat in stunned silence within the confines of her cubicle.

So she was right. They *were* all making fun of her. She didn't move, listening as they clicked their compact mirrors shut and finished perfecting each other's hair and makeup. After what felt like a lifetime, they finally walked out, leaving her behind in her lonely cubicle. As the click of the closing door echoed off the tiles, the tears Gloria had been holding back rushed to the surface, overwhelming her as her body convulsed with quiet sobs.

I tried. I really tried.

Gloria rubbed her eyes and rummaged through her handbag for her phone, barely able to see the screen through the veil of tears. She typed out a text to Greg with trembling fingers, pushing send before she could change her mind.

> I'm not feeling well. I'll
> take a taxi home.

Returning her phone to her bag, Gloria's eye was caught by the black and white card she had stashed there almost a week ago. She took it out and brushed her thumb over Meryl Hoffman-Mills's phone number. Within seconds she was typing out another message.

I'll do it.

◆———•●◆●•———◆

'A bit overdressed for fishin', aren't you?'

Gloria's eyes fluttered open, and she squinted at the dazzling sunlight which met her gaze. She wasn't sure how long she'd been asleep, but judging by the height of the sun in the sky, it couldn't have been long; it still was only mid-afternoon. She sat up and brushed the grass from her arms. The river ahead of her intensified the glare of the sun. She blinked, wondering if she had dreamed the voice which had awoken her.

'I wouldn't recommend it barefoot, neither.'

Gloria twisted to look behind her, shielding her eyes with her hand. Standing over her, silhouetted against the blazing sun, was a tall, broad-shouldered man. He seemed to be wearing workman's clothes, and he smiled at her with a broad grin framed by rough stubble. Gloria couldn't help but be relieved that it wasn't someone from the party. Lying comatose on the riverbank, stilettos strewn next to her on the ground, she wasn't exactly projecting the image of a well-to-do wife of one of their colleagues.

'Ha, no, I'm not exactly fishing. I'm just...having a break.' Gloria struggled to her feet, wrestling with the tight cocktail dress which didn't allow for easy movement, and faced the man directly. 'I'm, er, not used to this kind of party.'

For some reason, she didn't feel embarrassed admitting her discomfort to this stranger. There was something comforting and familiar about him.

'Ah, you're with one o' them?' He jerked his head towards the house. 'Should've guessed it from the dress, but I saw you lyin' on the ground and thought I'd check you were okay. Not injured or ill or nothin'.'

Gloria was touched; she doubted anyone in the gardens had even noticed she had gone, and here was a complete stranger, making sure she was all right.

'That's very kind. Thank you.' She smiled. 'But I'm fine. Just needed some fresh air, I suppose.'

She glanced back over at the river. Its shining surface lacked the power and intensity of the sea she had so revered in her youth, but it possessed an innate magic nonetheless. She took in a deep breath. The air had an intoxicating scent of fresh earth, beds of reeds and freshly mown grass. God, it was good to be close to nature. Not the well-tended, structured lawns and flower beds back at home, but genuine, authentic nature. It was wild and real, and Gloria loved it.

'Yep, it's much better out here.' The man's voice brought Gloria's attention back to him, but when she turned, she saw he was still looking out over the river, his soft blue eyes focused on the water. It was in that moment that Gloria realised why he seemed so familiar. He reminded her of Elias.

'Do you come here often?' Gloria asked, and immediately regretted her choice of words. 'Sorry, I don't mean to sound like I'm chatting you up!' she added, already getting flustered.

The man laughed, turning back to her with a smirk. 'Don't worry. I assumed you were attached to one of the suits in there.' He pointed a thumb back towards the house, and Gloria nodded. 'Harry Stubbs, plumber. Nice to meet you.'

Gloria took the hand he offered and shook it, enjoying Harry's easygoing nature. It was a breath of fresh air after the suffocating pressure of the party. 'Gloria Harrison, housewife and...artist, I suppose.'

'You don't sound very sure.' Harry's response sounded like a question, and Gloria wasn't sure how to respond. She didn't really feel qualified to call herself an artist, but introducing herself as only a housewife felt wrong somehow. Like she was selling herself short.

'Well, it's just a hobby,' she said, trying not to sound awkward. 'But I love it. I spend most of my days painting.'

'Sounds a damn sight better than sticking your arms down toilets and plug 'oles all day!'

Gloria began to laugh, but her amusement was short-lived as a cold voice cut across their genial conversation, grinding it to a sudden halt.

'Gloria.'

The word was sharp and laced with warning. Gloria looked over Harry's shoulder and saw Greg standing by the driveway of the house, his face thunderous. She glanced from him to the man she had been enjoying a friendly conversation with, unsure how best to react. Greg's usual charming exterior was nowhere to be found, replaced by a figure of steely hostility, and Gloria felt reluctant to approach him. He was her husband, her protector, but in that moment she felt afraid. She was rooted to the ground, her feet lead as a voice in her head whispered at her to run. As if in answer, Greg walked swiftly to where Gloria and Harry were standing and grabbed her roughly by the wrist.

'It's about time we were going home,' he said coolly, with a sidelong glance in Mr Stubbs's direction. Gloria barely had time to scoop up her forgotten shoes before she was dragged off towards the waiting Mercedes. She offered an apologetic smile to Harry, who remained on the grass, concern creasing his gentle features. Greg's grip on Gloria's arm was uncomfortably tight, and she struggled to keep up with his brisk pace. He ignored her protestations as he pulled her across the driveway, her bare feet scraping painfully on the gravel.

When they reached the car, Greg virtually threw Gloria into the passenger seat before pacing around to the driver's seat and climbing in.

'What the fuck do you think you're doing?' he spat, turning to face his wife, eyes blazing with fury.

Gloria recoiled at the venom in his voice and the ferocity of his question. She had barely begun to stammer out a response when Greg cut her off.

'And who the hell was that?'

'Just a-a friendly worker from the house,' Gloria managed to stutter. 'I was just having a break from the party.'

'A break from what?' Greg threw up a hand in frustration and leaned in close to Gloria, his right hand gripping the steering wheel so tightly his knuckles started to pale. 'From free food and champagne? From interesting conversations with my colleagues and friends? From having to make an effort for once in your fucking life?'

'Now that's not fair!' Gloria fired back, stung by his last question. 'I always—'

'You're always showing me up, that's what you're always doing.' Greg leaned in even closer, his face now only inches from hers. 'Do you know how important the clients are at this party? I bring you here to show off my *darling* wife, and you wander off to chat up some labourer by the river! Do you know how stupid you've made me look? How embarrassing this is? Do you?'

Gloria shrank back into the car seat, taken aback by Greg's tirade. Her throat tightened, and when she tried to reply, she could only muster a choked sob. Greg shook his head in disgust and started the engine. They drove home in silence.

The journey back to the house was fraught with a tension Gloria had never experienced before. She felt suffocated by the very air around her, her head aching from the pressure. Her fingers sat interlaced on her lap, knuckles white from the force required to stop her hands from shaking. Greg could be stern with her sometimes, occasionally losing his temper, but he had never been this angry before.

On reaching the end of the drive, Greg got out of the car without a word, slammed his door and strode quickly into the house. Gloria eventually followed, still barefoot as her heels lay in the foot well of the car, long forgotten. She barely noticed the sharp gravel of the driveway digging into her feet as she tiptoed into the house and quietly slipped through the door, her heart hammering against her ribs.

She padded through to the kitchen, hoping to calm her nerves with something from the wine fridge, but froze in the doorway when she saw Greg hunched over the breakfast bar, a crystal glass of whisky already in his hand. The ice cubes clinked softly as he slowly swirled his drink, head bowed as if in contemplation. For several long moments, Gloria didn't move, unsure how to proceed. He was breathing heavily, his back rising and falling in deep, ragged movements. If he'd noticed her presence, he didn't make it apparent.

Gloria turned to retreat as Greg finally spoke, his words quiet but hard. 'Don't ever embarrass me like this again. Do you hear me?' His eyes remained on the counter in front of him, and he took a slow sip of the amber liquid in his hand.

'Greg, I-I'm sorry...I didn't think,' Gloria began, the words tumbling out of her mouth in a jumbled mess.

'That's the problem,' Greg cut in, coldly. 'You never think.'

He looked up at her now, eyes dark and threatening, and Gloria shrank back against the doorframe. She had never seen Greg like this, and it sent a shiver down her spine. She took an uncertain step towards him, desperately hoping she could quell his temper. 'I tried, Greg, I really did.'

His laugh was harsh, and a painful scowl crossed his lips. 'You *tried*.' His voice dripped with sarcasm. He moved closer to Gloria, his face distorting into a vicious sneer. She soon regretted her approach, and for the first time in their marriage, she felt uneasy being in close proximity to her husband. The hairs on the back of her neck rose with each step he took.

'What exactly did you try? Copious glasses of booze? Shagging the help?'

Gloria bristled at that. She may not be perfect, but she had never once been unfaithful to him; to anyone. 'How... how dare you say that? I haven't ... I would never—'

'You can take the slut out of Amsterdam, I suppose...' Greg took another sip from his glass, chuckling to himself as he swallowed. 'I brought you here to give you a better life, but it seems you're determined to sabotage my efforts at every turn, Gloria. Is it too much to ask for a little gratitude? A little loyalty to the man you married?'

'I-I have always been grateful, you know that,' she stammered. 'You don't understand—'

'Oh, I understand perfectly, no mistake about that. Now, go to bed. I don't want to look at you anymore.'

'But—'

Gloria screamed as the whiskey glass collided with the doorframe and shattered, showering her with shards of sparkling wet crystal. She stood frozen in shock, eyes firmly fixed on the man who had thrown it at her, the husband she'd devoted her life to. Now, it was as if she was looking at a stranger, and he frightened her.

CHAPTER EIGHT

Gloria didn't move from under the covers until she heard Greg's car rolling down the driveway the following morning. Unsurprisingly, he hadn't come to bed last night, and Gloria was hit with a pang of sadness as she realised that had actually been a relief. Remembering the sheer fury in his eyes sent a fresh stab of anxiety through Gloria's stomach, and her chest tightened. His words echoed in her mind.

It seems you're determined to sabotage my efforts at every turn.

Had she really behaved so poorly yesterday? Perhaps she had left the party for longer than she had originally intended to but, after all, Greg had left her alone with those three dreadful women. What had he expected her to do? She sat up and shook her head slowly. Lately, she didn't seem able to please Greg no matter what she did. Maybe she never would. Maybe that was the problem.

With a gloomy sigh, Gloria threw off the covers and wandered across the room to the en suite. She needed a long, hot shower to wash away the last remnants of the previous night. As she stepped into the large glass cubicle and let the water rain down on her, she gradually felt her anxiety ease and begin to melt away. Having grown up in an environment where hot water was an infrequent extravagance, she still considered times like these a luxury. Greg had actually laughed as she gawked during her first tour of the house, not understanding that this way of life was a whole different world to the one she had grown up in.

Having rinsed herself clean of last night's unpleasantness, Gloria emerged into the bedroom in a cloud of steam, ready to face another day. Greg had overreacted last night, she was sure of it, and she wasn't going to spend another second obsessing about it. She had a gallery show to prepare for, after all; she wasn't going to spend the day cowering in bed.

◆——— • ● ◆ ● • ——— ◆

By late morning, Gloria was back in her studio, overalls on, hair scraped up and out of her face and poised to lose herself in a new piece of art. Since moving back to the UK, painting had become more and more of a necessity rather than a desire, and after Greg's outburst last night she needed this escape more than ever.

Casting her eyes over the blank canvas before her, Gloria's mind began to swim with vivid colours and shifting shapes. Crashing waves of cerulean and jade, a dazzling vermillion sunset framed by streaks of russet cloud, and a rich, velvet sky fading into inky black. The home she shared with Greg may be stark and devoid of life, but here in her world, there was a kaleidoscope of colour.

Flushed with fresh inspiration, Gloria reached out and grabbed at her pot of pencils, keen to sketch out her vision before it was lost to the ethers of her mind. What she found were blunted stubs of wood and graphite, overused in her recent flurry of activity, and now utterly useless.

'Damn it!' she cursed, frustration seeping into her voice.

She knew she couldn't hold on to a new idea for long, so she frantically scrabbled around the untidy, haphazard room in search of a forgotten new pencil she was sure must be around here somewhere. After several frenzied minutes, she was still empty-handed. Exasperated, she wandered out into the cool garden and looked up at the house. The only other place where she might find what she needed had always been off-limits to her: Greg's study.

◆——— • ● ◆ ● • ——— ◆

Gloria's stomach clenched as she padded upstairs to cross the boundary into Greg's private sanctum. It had never been an issue before – Gloria had little to no interest in snooping through Greg's work papers or client lists – so she had accepted his request to keep out without question. In previous weeks, Gloria might have taken a cab to town to pick up some new supplies, but she had work to do and didn't want to lose momentum. Besides, she still bristled from Greg's behaviour the night prior, so right now she had few reservations about trespassing into his hideout. If anything, Gloria felt a slight thrill rush through her as she reached for the doorknob; Greg's work had always been his priority, after all, so why shouldn't she take a peek at it?

She turned the knob and stepped forward, aware she was breaking Greg's trust, but in this moment, not caring whatsoever. The study looked much as Gloria had imagined it. Below the window sat a sleek silver desk sporting a painfully neat stack of moleskin notebooks and a metal set of shelves containing various pieces of paperwork. Gloria wasn't at all surprised to see a large, black leather chair towering behind the desk. It looked almost like a throne and seemed to fill the entire room.

Gloria stood in the doorway, slowly scanning the room for where Greg might keep his stationery. Unlike her, Greg didn't have pots of drawing utensils scattered about; the room was strictly organised with everything in its designated place. The walls held vast, steel cabinets which Gloria was certain were locked, and the only hint at disorganisation was the opened boxes of shiny corporate catalogues by the side of the desk. She supposed Greg had been checking through them. She was about to give up and head back downstairs when something caught her eye in one of the open boxes.

What?

Her eyes fell on a very familiar model smiling up at her from the front cover of the nearest catalogue stack. She had long, curly red hair and large blue eyes. She had a pensive expression and wasn't looking at the camera, perhaps unaware she was being photographed at all.

Holy shit.

It was her.

No, no, it can't be. I'm imagining things. Gloria's heart hammered against her rib cage as she knelt down to pick up the catalogue on the top of the pile with trembling hands. Her chest tightened as her fingers closed around the spine and she raised the glossy cover to her face.

There was no mistaking it. The woman on the cover was

Gloria, the photo apparently captured in secret during a social event Greg had taken her to almost a year ago; Gloria recognised the red evening gown that Greg had bought for her. *He'd said it was a gift,* she thought sourly. However, as her eyes passed over the title emblazoned across the top of the cover, the unapproved use of her image was no longer Gloria's primary concern. As her brain began to process the large, bold letters, her blood ran cold.

GENISOLVE: ARCHITECTS OF THE GENOME

RARE AND EXCLUSIVE DNA SAMPLES FOR OPTIMAL OFFSPRING

Gloria's heart pounded in her chest, and before she could stop herself, she was flipping through the pages with frantic fingers, quickly scanning every photo before moving on. There was an astonishing array of men and women scattered throughout the pages, each with a tagline highlighting their special trait of interest, be it their height, figure, skin tone, or even IQ. And there, on the centre page, was Gloria.

Make your child truly special with the rarest hair and eye combination in the world, exclusive to Genisolve.

Gloria felt sick.

Exclusive. The word echoed through her mind, resonating painfully, and it took Gloria a few seconds to realise why it stung so acutely. The realisation hit her like a freight train. It was exclusive because she was married to Greg. It was exclusive because he had tied her to him forever, so she could fritter away her days in blissful ignorance, unaware that her looks, her features, her very identity were being replicated elsewhere to fill the pockets of sleazy businessmen and their shareholders.

Glancing back into the box, she saw the same photo replicated on the next cover, and had no doubt that every catalogue in these boxes featured her unknowing, smiling face. The thought made her want to vomit.

CHAPTER NINE

At the sound of Greg's Mercedes creeping up the driveway, Gloria snapped out of her stupor and sat bolt upright. Was it that time already? She had been on the floor of Greg's study for hours, numb, her body overcome with horror and disbelief at what she had discovered. Trying to keep her breathing quiet, she cocked her ear up to listen, and soon heard Greg's shoes casually crunching up the driveway towards the house.

'Shit!'

She scrambled to her feet and dashed out of the room, barely remembering to close the door behind her as the front door swung open downstairs, announcing Greg's entrance. Gloria was about to head downstairs when she realised she still held the Genisolve catalogue, tightly grasped between her shaking fingers. Holding her breath, she tiptoed across the landing towards the master bedroom, hoping her clumsy feet wouldn't betray where she was fleeing from. Now she knew why Greg kept his study off-limits, Gloria could only imagine how he would react to finding her in there, especially after what she saw last night.

Gloria had just reached the stairs when Greg appeared in the kitchen doorway. She froze, throwing her hand behind her back to hide the catalogue. Her mouth went dry as she silently waited for Greg's next move, her mind racing as she tried and failed to figure out what to say should she be discovered. The seconds seemed to drag on forever, and still, Gloria didn't move. Her breathing resumed as Greg failed to notice her presence and sauntered across the hallway into the living room, an opened bottle of beer in his hand. Gloria's legs nearly gave way in relief as she dashed into the safety of her bedroom.

Without thinking, Gloria ran up to her dresser and stuffed the catalogue into the top drawer, turning it face down, so she didn't have to look at it ever again. She avoided her reflection at the best of times, having never felt positive about her looks. When she first escaped to Europe, she had even dyed her hair brunette in a futile attempt to lose her old self, to sever her family ties and start afresh. However, it had soon become apparent she couldn't keep up with it, and by the time she met Greg, her red curls were back in full force. *He always loved my hair.* The thought repulsed her.

As she turned away from the dresser, she caught sight of her reflection in the window. She grimaced; her eyes were red and swollen from tears she couldn't even remember crying, and black smears of mascara trailed down the sides of her face. She stumbled on unsteady feet into the en suite and numbly washed her face in the basin. Raising her head to look in the mirror, she scowled at the woman looking back at her. She had always wondered why a handsome, successful man such as Greg was interested in a screw-up like her. Now she knew why, and it was staring her straight in the face. This had been his motivation all along. He had looked her in the eyes on their wedding day and sworn his love to her, all the while planning to exploit her for his own gain.

And now she had to go downstairs and face him.

Gloria's face contorted in revulsion, and she almost didn't reach the toilet in time before she threw up what little contents were left in her stomach.

'Hit the wine a little early today?'

Gloria froze, trying not to react. Greg's very presence made her skin crawl, but she wasn't ready to confront him yet. At that moment, she wasn't sure if she ever could.

'Just a bug, I think,' she muttered into the toilet bowl, desperately hoping Greg wouldn't press the matter any further.

'I sincerely hope not,' Greg answered coolly. There was an edge to his voice which suggested he was not over last night's argument yet. 'You've got dinner to make.'

◆———— • ● ◆ ● • ————◆

Gloria took the pizza out of the oven and cut it into slices with trembling hands. She had been relieved that something so simple to prepare was already in the freezer; she couldn't think straight enough to make anything more complicated. Part of her was disgusted that she continued to serve Greg as his faithful housewife, but she was so numb with shock she was running on autopilot. Her hands continued to prepare dinner for her husband while her brain screamed at her to *do* something, anything.

But what could she realistically do? Greg had dominion over everything in Gloria's life: her finances, her home, even her daughter. Gloria's chest tightened at the thought of Iris. Greg was the reason she could go to International School, and his generous support payments meant she and Elias could live a comfortable life in Amsterdam, something they never would have had if Gloria hadn't travelled back to the UK and married Greg. She couldn't take that all away from Iris. Sixteen years ago, Gloria gave herself a mission to provide for her daughter the way she had never been provided for growing up, and she did not intend to fail her.

Swallowing the bile rising in her throat, she put the plate of pizza onto a wooden tray and carried it through to the living room. Greg didn't acknowledge her at first; he was focused on the television on the wall opposite his brown leather recliner. Gloria silently placed the tray on his lap and took her usual place on the sofa beside his chair.

Greg studied his dinner for a moment, and looked over at Gloria, his forehead creased in confusion. 'You're not eating?' he asked, his voice somewhat lighter than it had been upstairs.

'I told you,' she replied quietly without looking at him. 'I'm not well.'

Greg reached over from his chair to place a hand on Gloria's arm. Try as she might, she couldn't help but recoil at his touch.

'You're angry.' He shifted in his seat so he could look Gloria directly in the face, but she couldn't look at him, let alone speak.

'I'm sorry.' The sincerity in his voice forced Gloria to meet his gaze. He'd adopted his usual caring expression, but Gloria couldn't take it seriously, not now that she knew his secret.

'I overreacted yesterday,' he continued, brown eyes shining in the light from the TV. 'I realise that now. I just love you so much, and it hurt that you snubbed my colleagues who were dying to see you. I shouldn't have shouted at you. I know that.'

GLORIA

'And?' Gloria probed, his apology doing nothing to quell the disgust she felt for the man looking into her eyes.

'And I'm sorry I threw the glass. That was uncalled for.' *So, that's it. That's all he's sorry for.* 'I hope you forgive me.'

Greg continued to look into Gloria's eyes for a moment, his face the picture of earnest sincerity, before turning away to resume watching the TV, the matter apparently settled despite Gloria's lack of response. She watched Greg eat his dinner in silence, seemingly certain that everything was now fine between them. As she observed his smug indifference to her, Gloria knew with increased clarity that things could not continue as they had before. She had to find out more.

CHAPTER TEN

The sudden lurch of the train as it pulled into a station nearly sent Gloria crashing into the wall of the small toilet cubicle. She cursed her decision to do this on the way into London, but she couldn't risk Greg walking in on her at home. Grinning at her reflection in the small, grubby mirror, she tucked the last few remaining curls into the short, black wig and stepped back to admire her new appearance. It had been pure luck that her dress-up box had survived the journey back to the UK from Amsterdam; Greg's car had been easily filled, and many of her belongings had been abandoned with Elias and Iris, or simply thrown away.

Despite everything, Gloria couldn't help but smile as she smoothed down the wig in the mirror. While she and Katie were struggling to make ends meet on the continent, dressing up as their ridiculous alter egos was one of the few ways they could afford to have fun. Gloria would be a sophisticated, mysterious artist while Katie strutted the streets as a blonde Hollywood star. It was silly. The outfits were cheap and less than convincing, but those days were some of the happiest of Gloria's life.

A wave of sadness washed over her as she considered how different she had become. Her life with Greg in the verdant Surrey countryside had seemed like a dream come true when it was first proposed to her, but only now did she realise how hollow it had turned out to be.

She didn't want to dwell on that and pushed those thoughts to the back of her mind as she returned to fixing her wig in the mirror. Turning her head from side to side, she studied her appearance. With her red curls hidden from view and her face framed by a sharp, dark bob, she looked like an entirely different person. She felt like an undercover spy taking part in a covert operation, and a spark of confidence ignited within her, which she hadn't experienced for a long time. Her fantasy was abruptly cut short when the chime of the train's intercom system crackled through a speaker behind her head.

'We are now approaching London Waterloo, where the service will terminate.'

Gloria took a deep breath and placed a large pair of sunglasses over her eyes.

'Here we go.'

Gloria's heart pounded as she stared up at the vast, shining building in front of her. Genisolve were clearly profiting very well from their latest venture, and Gloria couldn't help but feel intimidated by the sense of wealth and power which radiated from their headquarters. The building was painfully clinical, all glass and sharp corners, absurdly tall windows gleaming in the sunlight.

Greg had never spoken much about his office, insisting

Gloria wouldn't find it interesting. She had believed him, of course. Now she understood it was just to keep her from knowing too much about what his company was actually doing. She allowed her anger to boil to the surface a little; she would need it to give her the courage to go through with her plan.

Rolling back her shoulders and adopting an air of grandeur that felt entirely alien to her, Gloria sauntered towards the entrance. Before she passed through the revolving door, she took a moment to check her reflection. Her wig was still perfectly in place, and she'd managed to travel across London on the tube without creasing her dress too much. It was a slinky purple number which she had only worn once at Greg's request. It had been a particularly expensive birthday present from him, and Gloria had chosen it as her best chance at looking like a wealthy socialite; the type of person who might pay for a designer baby.

Genisolve had clearly decided to carry their clinical design preferences into the interior of the building, as well. The revolving door opened into the end of a long atrium which ran along the front of the building, a wall of glass on one side and the opposite side made up of a gleaming white wall, empty aside from an extremely large steel version of their logo, a rather unimaginative "G" and "S" separated by a single strand of DNA. Aside from the sleek, white reception desk directly in front of Gloria, the atrium itself contained several small groups of black and white sharp-edged tables and chairs, all perfectly lined up in a symmetrical pattern. They were sparsely populated by a handful of executive types, all drinking coffee and peering into their laptop screens. The expansive, rectangular windows in the ceiling let in a vast amount of sunlight which glittered on every surface. Gloria was glad of the light; it gave her an excuse to keep her sunglasses on for as long as possible.

As she approached the reception desk, a tall, slender, blonde woman with features almost as angular as the surroundings looked up at her. 'Hello, and welcome to Genisolve. How can I help?' Her voice sounded almost robotic, as if saying the same phrase repeatedly for years and had caused the words to lose all meaning.

Gloria tried to channel the false confidence her alter ego imbued her with. 'Ah, hello, hello.' She made her best attempt at an upper-class accent, whilst making it clear her greeting was not particularly sincere. 'A friend of mine is a client of yours – not that she'd admit to it in our social circle, of course!' She barked an unsure laugh, but if the receptionist was thinking anything of it, her blank expression gave nothing away. 'She tells me you are offering some interesting, premium products for starting a new family.'

At this, the receptionist's eyes widened with recognition. Gloria held her breath, unsure if she had been too forward and already blown it.

'Oh, yes, right.' The receptionist's voice lowered, and she glanced left to right to check no one was within earshot. 'Of course, ma'am. I'll send a call out to our Director of New Accounts who will talk you through your options. Please, take a seat.'

She gestured to her right, and Gloria tried to hide her relief as she entered the atrium and took a seat at the nearest table. Still, it wasn't over yet, and her stomach roiled with anxiety. She sank back into the rather uncomfortable, hard chair and had to suppress a jump as the woman's voice unexpectedly returned.

'Can I get you a drink while you wait?'

Gloria named the first remotely interesting drink she could think of. 'Oh, Earl Grey tea, please. Unsweetened.' Gloria assumed even the high-end clients of Genisolve wouldn't ask for wine or champagne this early in the day.

'Of course, right away.'

Gloria barely noticed the tea as it arrived; she was busy scanning the atrium for any sign of Greg. She might pass unnoticed by his colleagues, who had only met her once or twice, but Greg saw her every day, and a cheap wig and a pair of sunglasses might not be enough to prevent her from standing out. Besides, he'd bought her this dress. Granted, she'd only worn it very briefly years ago, but Greg had a sharp eye and a good memory.

It was to Gloria's immense relief that the young man who eventually approached her was someone she didn't remotely recognise. She only hoped the feeling was mutual. After all, she didn't know how far those new catalogues had circulated. The man smiled as he reached Gloria's table and offered his hand to greet her.

'Welcome to Genisolve.' He grinned, displaying a mouth of perfect, white teeth. 'I'm Sebastian, New Accounts Director. It's very good to meet you, Ms.?'

'Rowbotham.' Gloria took his hand and gave it a gentle shake. 'Sophia Rowbotham.'

She had stolen each half of the name from neighbours who seemed to be the type of women Gloria was trying to emulate. It seemed apt.

'I'm told you are interested in some of our more exclusive products.' Sebastian glanced over his shoulder before leaning in closer. 'Why don't we go somewhere more private and discuss your needs?'

◆ —— • ● ◆ ● • —— ◆

When Sebastian finally left Gloria alone to "think over her options", she slumped back into the plush, black armchair and let the tension drop from her shoulders, able to temporarily drop her Sophia Rowbotham persona at last. He had been the typical charming salesman so far, leading her through the building's gleaming white corridors whilst giving a full run-through of Genisolve's rich history of scientific excellence and life-saving research. Of course, that was all a preamble to where their real big profits came from: peddling DNA.

Gloria stared at the plastic folder sitting on the table in front of her. She couldn't bear to open it. Listening to Sebastian talk through the process the first time had been more than enough. Many of the examples he'd shown her were also in the catalogue she'd seen already, and Gloria couldn't help but wonder if those people were as ignorant as she'd been about her part in this venture. Some of the others were young, no more than children really; that had been particularly unsettling.

Sebastian had said he'd be ten minutes or so, and it dawned on Gloria that this might be her only chance to find something out about Genisolve beyond the corporate sales pitch she'd been given so far. She'd been told a good story, of course, but it had all been about the benefits of having complete confidence in your child's future. The ethics of the process had been sidestepped entirely. Gloria assumed their regular clientele weren't typically troubled by such things, and yet she was the one continually looked down upon. *Hypocrites.* She glanced at the closed door. Technically, no one had told her to stay in the room, but no doubt there was an expectation she wouldn't wander off.

Tiptoeing to the door, she opened it a crack and peered down the corridor. It was empty, for now. She had tried to take note of the rooms they passed on their way to the consulting room, nodding along to Sebastian with faux interest all the while, but every room and corridor in this place looked identical, and there was no telling what was behind each door. Still, she couldn't stand not knowing anything any longer, so, with no plan whatsoever, she stepped out into the corridor and walked quickly in a random direction.

Trying to maintain a confidence that suggested she was supposed to be there, Gloria strode down the corridor, sneaking glances into every office which had a window or open door. Much to her frustration, every room seemed to be occupied, and she wasn't quite brave enough to continue the charade with more Genisolve employees. She could only push her luck so far, and she knew it. Time was slipping away, however, and Gloria started to wonder whether to turn back.

She was poised to head back the way she had come when she heard footsteps echoing behind her. A quick glance over her shoulder revealed a smartly dressed woman looking at a clipboard heading in Gloria's direction. Her heart raced as she quickened her step and pushed on around the next corner.

Then she saw him.

Greg was just rounding the corner at the opposite end of the corridor, chatting away to a man Gloria didn't recognise. She froze in place, eyes wide with horror, knowing at any moment Greg could look forwards and spot her. God only knew what he would do then, and Gloria didn't want to find out.

Her mind raced. She couldn't go back and risk being stopped by the woman steadily catching up to where she stood, but she'd need a miracle to get by Greg unnoticed. Her heart pounded with such ferocity she was surprised she couldn't see it rising out of her chest. She had to think; she was wasting time. Every second she spent panicking, Greg took one step closer, and he could look up from his conversation at any moment.

Greg's companion raised his hand towards where she stood, and Gloria rushed through the nearest door in a blind panic – straight into the men's toilets.

Idiot!

She slowly turned on the spot, weighing up her options. She couldn't go back out into the corridor, not when she might crash straight into Greg. She could listen out for them passing by, but she felt vulnerable lingering in the middle of a room she definitely shouldn't be in. Gloria bit her bottom lip, paralysed with indecision, but her mind was made up for her as the door started to open inwards towards her. She barely had time to scramble into one of the cubicles and slam the door shut before she heard a familiar voice echoing off the tiles.

'It's going to be a big score, this one. Trust me.'

Gloria cringed at her husband's voice, wondering how she had ever fallen in love with this creep.

'She certainly impressed at the party,' the stranger answered.

Gloria held her breath, desperately hoping they wouldn't notice the occupied cubicle behind them as they stood at the urinal. She huddled as far away from the door as she could, just in case.

'Good, good. I was worried the stupid cow had blown it when she wandered off from the girls. But maybe it added to the feeling of exclusivity, that they only got to have a glimpse of the goods.' Greg let out a cruel laugh.

Gloria felt like she'd been punched in the stomach. It took all of her strength to hold herself upright.

'I'm not supposed to share this yet.' The other man lowered his voice, so Gloria had to strain to hear him. 'We have a few high-rolling clients lined up already. How soon can you bring in the samples?'

'Aha! Excellent!' Gloria thought she could hear Greg rubbing his hands together. 'The lab team are prepping the kits as we speak. I should be able to take them home next Friday, and then it'll be a matter of days – three at most.'

Gloria's body went stiff.

'You think it will be that easy?'

'Of course.' Greg laughed. 'She's fucking clueless and does pretty much whatever I tell her to. Don't worry. You'll have the samples within two weeks.'

Gloria didn't hear the two men leave the bathroom. She could hardly hear anything through the sound of her own heart pounding in her ears as she tried to hold back the hot, angry tears burning behind her eyes. Her legs had turned to jelly. She could hardly breathe, Greg's words spinning around in her mind.

Next Friday.

After a few minutes, she managed to steady herself and stagger out into the corridor, where she numbly walked back towards the consulting room.

'Oh, Ms Rowbotham! I thought we'd lost you!' Sebastian exclaimed as he rounded the nearest corner looking flushed, his relief at finding his potential client clear on his face.

'Oh...so sorry,' Gloria managed to get out. 'I had to use the restroom, and I got a little lost.'

'No problem, no problem. Now, let's talk about our wide range of flexible payment packages.'

Gloria didn't take in a single word, Sebastian's chatter going in one ear and out the other. What the people-pleasing salesman had to say was of minimal importance to her now. Her mind was entirely focused on one thought: she had to stop Greg.

CHAPTER ELEVEN

Gloria's phone shook in her hands as she read over the message she'd been redrafting all morning. After faking a migraine yesterday to minimise interaction with Greg, her head had been spinning with thoughts and ideas, all of which had culminated in this moment. If she pressed "Send", it would make her decision final, and she couldn't go back. Her heart pounded as she tapped the screen with a trembling finger.

> I need your help. I'm leaving Greg. There's too much to explain in a message, can we meet up soon? Got to get out ASAP.

There, she'd done it. She would lose everything, but she'd be free. Free from Greg's exploitation, at least, and that was enough. Gloria had wracked her brains all night, wondering who might be able to help her escape this situation, and only one name made sense: Katie. Her old friend had no ties to Greg, and so was the only person Gloria could trust to keep this from him. It had been a painful realisation that all of her friends here in Surrey had been introduced to her through Greg. Now she thought about it, she realised they weren't really friends at all, not in the true sense of the word. They were nothing more than acquaintances, members of Greg's social network who could keep Gloria busy when she demanded too much of Greg's attention. Her connections to her past had been carefully kept at arm's length; Greg had made sure of that.

The wait for Katie's reply was agonising. No doubt she was at work, unable to check her phone until lunchtime, but despite that logical explanation, Gloria couldn't stop herself from checking for a reply every few minutes. Her stomach churned, and half of her nails were bitten down to their beds by the time her phone finally vibrated with an incoming call.

'Glor? Look, I can't stay on long, I'm between meetings, but what's going on? Has something happened? Has he hurt you?'

'No, no, I'm okay.' Gloria tried to sound calmer than she felt. Did Katie really think Greg was capable of that? 'It's a long story, but I have to get out, Katie, and I don't have much time. I have to get out before next Friday.'

Katie was quiet for a moment. 'I'm sorry, but I'm not sure how much I can help.' Gloria's stomach dropped. She had been so sure her friend would support her. 'I'm in Paris with work for the next couple of weeks, trying to close out a major deal.'

The phone went silent, and Gloria felt the hope drain from her body. Katie's voice finally returned, full of concern for her friend.

'Can you get out here? If you can get a flight, I'm sure you could stay in my hotel room with me. It's pretty spacious, and work won't need to know.'

Gloria considered this for a moment, but she knew it wasn't possible. She hesitated, unable to find the words to explain it to Katie; she was too embarrassed.

'Glor, if you need money, I can send it to you. It's no trouble.'

Gloria squeezed her eyes shut, realisation hitting her. 'We only have joint accounts. Greg would see. He'd know I was leaving. God, how did I let myself get in this mess? I don't know what to do, I—'

'Calm down, calm down. Don't worry.' Katie could clearly hear the rising panic in Gloria's voice. Greg controlled all the finances in their relationship; Gloria had no hope of getting anywhere alone.

'Go to Meryl. Ask her if she can advance you the money for your paintings. She's a good person, Gloria. She'll help you, I'm sure of it. Look, I have to go, but I'm here if you need me. Just call me, and I'll do what I can. And Glor?'

'Yeah?'

'I'm so proud of you. You're doing the right thing.'

The phone beeped, and Katie was gone, back to her meeting and her busy schedule in Paris. Gloria couldn't resent her for that. She couldn't realistically expect Katie to drop everything and come over to rescue her, especially after she'd virtually cut her out of her life until recently. If Katie hadn't thought of her when she happened to come across Meryl at a work function, Gloria wouldn't have reconnected with her at all. Katie had proven herself to be the much better friend.

Meryl.

Would Meryl really be willing to help her? Yes, they'd gotten along well for that one afternoon, but she was a stranger. Gloria was just a potential artist for her gallery, probably one of many Meryl currently had lined up. Panic began to creep into her body, gripping at her chest. Had it been reckless to message Katie? Was she crazy to consider leaving Greg when he had control over every aspect of her life? She had no real plan, just a desperate hope someone would be able to help her. For a moment, Gloria considered messaging Katie again and telling her it was a mistake, that she had changed her mind, that she should forget everything.

And then she remembered what Greg had said about her – that she was "fucking clueless" and would bend to his will. He had laughed at her, knowing with absolute certainty she would do his bidding. The very thought of sticking by his side as he used her to bolster his bank account made her feel ill. She had to get out. If it meant begging Meryl for help, then so be it.

◆——— · ● ◆ ● · ——— ◆

Gloria fiddled with her skirt nervously, aware that her tea was going cold, forgotten on the table, but feeling too tense to drink it. To her relief, the café was quite busy, hopefully preventing any opportunity for their conversation to be over-heard. Perhaps she was just being paranoid, but she felt the need to constantly check over her shoulder. Greg had seemed thoroughly convinced by the excuse of coming into London for painting supplies, yet Gloria's shoulders itched with the feeling of being watched.

Meryl had been as amicable as Gloria remembered her on the phone, and agreed to her request to meet quite easily. It had been a much-needed stroke of good luck that she had an hour free the next day. Gloria only had one week to get her affairs in order before Greg would try to harvest her DNA, and she was adamant she would not let that happen under any circumstance. The very thought made her shudder.

Gloria's heart leapt when Meryl finally arrived, fashionably late in a sweeping black cape and matching Fedora. She offered a friendly wave to Gloria while she ordered at the counter, engaging in easy banter with the barista. The young man blushed, and for a fleeting moment, Gloria thought Meryl was flirting with him.

'Gloria, so good to see you!' Meryl exclaimed as she sat down with her coffee, leaning over to kiss Gloria on her cheek. 'How are you? You sounded a little panicked on the phone.'

Now Meryl was here, Gloria found herself tongue-tied. The last week or so had been such a rollercoaster that she hadn't processed any of it properly, and before she could get any words out, she burst into tears. Meryl didn't say anything, instead placing a soft hand on Gloria's arm and squeezing gently. Gloria's words came through as gasping sobs. 'I...I'm sorry, Meryl. I...'

'Take your time, dear,' Meryl soothed. 'Honestly, there's no rush.'

Then the words tumbled out. How Gloria was leaving Greg, that she only had a week to get out, how Katie had offered her a sanctuary in Paris but she couldn't afford the flights, how she desperately needed to sell her paintings, all of it. Well, almost. She didn't mention anything about *why* she had to leave. Gloria couldn't bring herself to vocalise it. She felt too ashamed.

Meryl was silent throughout, patiently nodding as Gloria spoke, never once interrupting or passing comment. Only when Gloria had finished and was quietly sniffling into a tissue did she speak.

'Gloria,' she began in a calm, measured tone. 'Am I right that you're asking if I can put some money towards your paintings in advance so you can get out of your house next week?'

Gloria didn't look up. She felt pathetic. 'Yes. I'm sorry. It's rude. I shouldn't have—'

'Gloria,' Meryl cut her off and moved her head so she could meet Gloria's gaze. Her eyes were warm with compassion. 'Of course I will help you.'

Gloria sat upright, taken aback by the older woman's quick offer of assistance. She had grown so used to having to beg and persuade Greg to do anything for her, she had expected more effort to be needed. 'Really? You're sure?'

'Darling, your paintings are stunning, and I was planning on snapping up a good number of them eventually, anyway. And even if they were ghastly, I would still help you. I don't know what this man has done to you, but I can see in your eyes that you have to get out, and I trust that it's for a very good reason. Now,' She handed Gloria a ten-pound note, a mischievous smile spreading across her face. 'Order two slices of chocolate cake, and we'll start working on a plan.'

◆———— • ● ◆ ● • ———— ◆

When the taxi pulled up outside the house, Greg's Mercedes was already parked on the drive. Gloria frowned and looked at her phone; it was only three-thirty. Greg was home early. Gloria paid the driver, grabbed her bags and stood rooted in place as the car slowly pulled away. She needed a few minutes outside to slip back into wife mode.

'Greg? Are you home?' she called as she walked through the door, keeping her voice as light and casual as she could manage.

The hallway was empty, the house eerily quiet. *He must be working in his study*, Gloria thought, making her way into the kitchen. She dropped her bags on the breakfast bar and pulled out the first bottle she spotted on the wine rack. Right now, with her nerves fraying into pieces, she just wanted a drink. She was pouring out her first glass of Merlot when a cold voice startled her so much she nearly dropped the bottle.

'You're late.'

'Oh, Greg! You made me jump!'

Gloria looked up at her husband, standing in the doorway, his expression unreadable. A moment of silence passed, with his only shift in features a slight raise of one eyebrow as if he was waiting for a response to a question.

'I told you I was going into the city for supplies.' She gestured to the bags. Greg walked over to the counter slowly and opened each bag one by one, peering inside with a distinct frown on his face.

'Not much to show for a full day of shopping.' Greg looked at Gloria, his eyes hard with suspicion. 'What else were you doing?'

'Well,' Gloria forced herself to retain eye contact, though she desperately wanted to look away. 'You know how indecisive I am! It took me almost an hour just to decide which pencils to get, and then I wondered whether to scrap pencils altogether and switch to charcoal. But they'd run out of charcoal at the first shop, so I had to take the tube to Oxford Street—'

'Okay, okay,' Greg interrupted, stepping back and waving a hand to stop Gloria's rambling. 'I get it. God, how do you women cope with being so scatterbrained?' He laughed, shaking his head, and wandered over to the fridge to retrieve a beer.

Gloria shrugged and forced out a laugh which she hoped was at least somewhat convincing. 'Lucky for me I have all the time in the world to shop, I suppose.'

'Lucky for you, I have enough money in the bank to pay for your hobbies.' Greg laughed in return, and the tension finally dropped from the room. Greg was satisfied, for now at least.

Gloria watched as he disappeared from view, taking his drink upstairs. From the sound of his footsteps, he was heading into his study to work. Ordinarily, this would be fine with her, but knowing he was probably in there pitching her saliva or skin cells or God knows what to his wealthy clientele made her feel sick to her stomach. She threw the wine down her throat in one swallow, the warmth of the alcohol spreading through her chest and soothing her. She immediately filled a second glass.

CHAPTER TWELVE

Six days left.

Gloria and Meryl had decided on one critical action she needed to complete to have any chance of following through on their plan: she had to retrieve her passport.

Gloria hadn't given it a second thought when she'd allowed Greg to store all of their documents in his safe box. After all, they lived in an affluent area, and their house was a prime target for burglars. Now, however, Greg held not only the key to their most important documents, but also to Gloria's freedom. She had been so fixated on getting money together to fly out to Katie that the availability of her passport hadn't even occurred to her. Thankfully, Meryl's level-headedness had saved Gloria from making that mistake too late.

Unsurprisingly, Greg hadn't told Gloria where he kept the key to the safe box, and in truth, Gloria had never seen him use it. She knew she couldn't ask him for the key outright – she'd never cared before, why would she now? It did cross her mind to ask Greg a question about her passport under the guise of preparing for her birthday trip, but the last thing she wanted was to draw attention to it, and for him to later realise it had disappeared. No, she had to find the key.

Once Greg had left for work, Gloria waited for five minutes to be certain he was gone before beginning her search. Greg kept his possessions immaculately tidy, so Gloria knew she had to be careful to put anything she touched perfectly back in place.

She started in the bedroom, cautiously opening Greg's set of drawers one by one in search of the key. She was slowed by the neatness of each drawer; Gloria knew she couldn't replicate the perfect folding of his socks and underwear, so had to painstakingly lift each item out to look underneath.

'God, if this man gets any more anal, he'll be a walking arsehole,' Gloria muttered to herself.

She opened the uppermost drawer of Greg's bedside table, and her stomach flipped as she spotted an item that was definitely out of place: a bright pink lace bra. Gloria lifted it out and looked it over, but she didn't recognise it. She supposed it could have been a gift he hadn't got around to giving her, but the colour and fabric certainly weren't her usual style. She was about to stuff it back into the drawer when something else caught her eye. There was a Polaroid lying face down in the drawer. She was almost certain Greg didn't own a Polaroid camera.

Reaching into the drawer, Gloria turned over the photograph and gasped, almost dropping it in shock. Her hand may have been shaking, but there was no doubt who was staring back at her in the image. Victoria, Greg's gorgeous blonde colleague, wearing the pink bra and matching underwear, and nothing else. But it was what was written along the bottom of the photo which turned Gloria's stomach to stone.

GLORIA

To keep you fired up when you're with the Mrs x

Gloria was mortified. So, Greg wasn't just exploiting her for money, he was also cheating on her, and with that arrogant, overbearing woman. She probably should have found this trivial, considering everything that had happened recently, but the pain cut through her chest like a knife. She and Greg didn't have the most passionate of marriages, that was true, but she had given everything to him, and had always thought he was satisfied. Now, Gloria she knew for certain she had been nothing but a business venture.

She stared at the photo as it began to crumple in her fingers. The threat of tears prickled behind her eyes as a new heat spread through her body, a heat Gloria hadn't felt in a long time. She wasn't devastated or crushed; she wasn't frightened or defeated. She was furious.

She had devoted herself to Greg. He'd promised her the world, and she'd fallen for it hook, line and sinker. She'd left behind a city she loved and her wonderful daughter, a daughter who was currently ignoring her because of *him*. He'd assured her it was for the best. He'd take care of them both, he'd provide for their future, he'd put Iris through school, the best school in Amsterdam, and all she had to do was go with him. Go with him and be an unwitting guinea pig for his twisted schemes.

Gloria looked at the bra still dangling from her fingers and flung it away from her, disgusted by Greg's betrayal. The offending item skimmed the top of the target drawer and crashed into the neatly arranged trio of aftershave bottles sitting atop Greg's bedside table, toppling them. One hadn't been closed fully and began to bleed its contents onto the polished wood.

'Shit! Shit! Shit!'

She pulled a pillow from the bed and frantically mopped up the liquid, but the more she rubbed, the more she stripped off the wood's finish. Despite her best efforts, there remained a distinct patch of raw wood in the centre of the perfectly lacquered surface. Exasperated, Gloria threw the pillow to one side and bit her lip as she stared at the mess she'd created. Greg didn't spend much time in the bedroom. Maybe she could rearrange the bottles and he wouldn't notice. She used the largest bottle to cover the mark, and placed the others roughly where she remembered them standing before. That would have to do.

She reached over to retrieve the bra, which had fallen behind the bedside table. However, when she tugged on it, the strap seemed to be caught on something. Gloria felt around the back of the table and could feel the strap wedged behind a piece of cold metal fastened to the wood with what felt like masking tape. She scratched at the tape with her fingers until she could dislodge the metal and free the bra. As she sat back on her knees to examine what she'd found, all thoughts of cheating husbands and usurping colleagues fell from her mind – it was a key.

Gloria's heart leapt. Finally, a stroke of luck. She carefully tucked the bra and photo back into the drawer, trying to smooth out the creases in the Polaroid as she did so. Her anger at Greg morphed into firm determination as she threw open his wardrobe to reveal the safe box nestled under a neat row of well-polished dress shoes. She allowed herself a small smile as the key slotted in perfectly. She opened the door, letting out a small sigh of relief as she spotted two passports sat atop a small stack of paperwork.

GLORIA

Gloria picked them both up, identified hers quickly and stuffed it into her handbag. She hesitated as she went to return Greg's passport to the safe. Part of her wanted to take it, to destroy it even, to punish Greg in some small way for everything he'd done to her. She ran her thumb over the golden writing, the temptation to rip it open and tear out the pages building within her. With a soft sigh, she placed it back on top of the pile of papers. No, she didn't want to be like that. Like him. She was better than that. She threw the safe box door closed and locked it before she could change her mind.

CHAPTER THIRTEEN

Five days left.

'I just can't decide. I think I'll have to buy them all.'

Gloria smiled over at Meryl, silhouetted against the bright afternoon sky as the sun shone through the studio windows.

'Please, Meryl, don't feel like you have to just to help me out. It's really—'

'Now, shush,' Meryl interrupted, waving a hand at her dismissively. 'I'm a frugal woman, and I don't buy anything unless I want it. These will look perfect in the North Gallery, with the backdrop of the Thames through the windows.'

Gloria beamed. Despite everything, she still couldn't quite believe that her paintings would finally be on display in a real, professional art gallery. It was thrilling.

'It's a dream come true,' she muttered softly. Meryl, however, glanced back at her with a look of sadness on her face. 'What's wrong?'

'Oh, I just hope you get to see the exhibition for yourself.' She placed a gentle hand on Gloria's arm. 'It will be such a shame if you don't come back to London because...well, because of him.' Meryl jerked her head towards the main house with a look of intense disapproval. Gloria hadn't explained the full extent of Greg's misdeeds to Meryl, but the older woman seemed to take an immediate dislike to Greg from what she had heard nonetheless. She explained it as being "an excellent judge of character".

Gloria considered her new friend for a moment. After all of the help and support she'd offered Gloria so far, Meryl was still concerned about her, and at that moment, it hit Gloria that she hadn't felt so cared for before. Her mother had seen her as little more than an annoyance, and Greg's affections had only been skin deep, but Gloria felt true warmth from Meryl, and it was almost overwhelming.

'Meryl, after everything you've done for me, I promise I will find a way to see it. Thank you, so very much.' Soft tears began to roll down Gloria's cheeks. She closed her eyes and melted into the embrace offered by her friend.

'Don't let anyone make you think you don't deserve to be happy,' Meryl said into her shoulder, squeezing her tight. 'Now, enough of the emotional breakthroughs. Let's get these canvases wrapped up!'

◆ —— • ● ◆ ● • —— ◆

It took the best part of the afternoon for Gloria and Meryl to wrap up the majority of the paintings in her studio, leaving only the unfinished pieces and some of Gloria's more senti-mental works behind. As Gloria picked up the last couple of canvases to bring into the house, she marvelled at how bare the studio now looked. She had grown used to surrounding herself with her work, escaping her suffocating life in the

house to this world of colour and vibrancy. Now it looked so...
empty. She supposed it was for the best – it would be easier to
leave this way.

Meryl was sat at the breakfast bar finishing off a cup of tea
when Gloria brought in the final paintings and stacked them
up by the door. Gloria had insisted she take care of all the
heavy lifting; it was the least she could do.

'My assistant is on his way to collect the paintings,' she
called, waving Gloria into the kitchen. 'Now, let me settle the
bill.'

As Gloria sat down beside her, Meryl drew a small
bundle of ten, twenty and fifty pound notes out of her
oversized handbag. Gloria's eyes widened – she hadn't
expected anything near that much! 'Meryl...are you sure?'
she stammered, unsure if she could accept such a generous
payment from someone who had given her so much already.

'It's a fair price, my dear.' Meryl insisted, pushing the
money into Gloria's hands. 'Now keep this out of sight and
don't keep it all in one place, just in case.'

'Thank you.' Gloria slipped the money into her handbag,
the smile dropping from her face as she glimpsed her phone
and something caught her eye which twisted her stomach
into a knot: two missed calls from Greg.

'Gloria...what is it?' She wordlessly held up the phone to
Meryl, whose brow creased with concern. 'Call him back. It's
most likely nothing.'

Gloria was about to return Greg's call when she noticed
a voicemail symbol flashing in the corner of the screen;
she'd received the message almost an hour ago. She called
the voicemail number and cringed as Greg's voice seeped
through the speaker.

'Hello, Gloria. I'm assuming you've forgotten to take your phone into your studio again, but I'm letting you know I'm coming home early. I thought we could go out for dinner, so I hope you haven't started cooking yet! See you soon. Bye.'

A beep signalled the end of the message, and Gloria hung up the phone.

Shit.

'He's on his way home!' Gloria shrieked, panic starting to spread through her body. 'We have to get the paintings out!'

Meryl nodded and retrieved her own phone from her bag, holding a finger up to indicate Gloria should wait while she made a call.

'Samuel? Where are you? Okay, good, get here as quickly as you can. We need to get packed up and gone ASAP, and I mean that. We'll be ready, just back straight up to the door.'

Meryl hung up and looked at Gloria, determination shining in her eyes. 'My assistant is almost here. Let's get these paintings outside so we can get them straight in the van and set off before hubby gets home.'

Meryl moved surprisingly quickly for someone in her mid-sixties, and before long, both women had stacked the wrapped canvases outside the house, awaiting Meryl's assistant's arrival. Gloria wrung her hands impatiently as the minutes slipped by, painfully aware that Greg was getting closer with every passing second.

She was surprised by how frightening the thought of discovery of her escape was. After all, couples split up all the time. She was entitled to leave if she wasn't happy. Even so, there was something about the idea of Greg figuring out what she was doing that was...threatening. Greg had shown how volatile he could be after the garden party, and Gloria knew in her gut he would not react well to being jilted.

As if sensing Gloria's unease, Meryl reached out and put an arm around Gloria's shoulders. 'Don't worry. He'll be here any second.'

It was a further five long minutes before a small white van bearing the words "Hofmann-Mills" finally appeared at the end of the driveway, slowly rolling towards the house. As instructed, the driver backed it right up to the door so Meryl and Gloria could slide the canvases directly into the back. Gloria didn't even have the chance to catch a glimpse of the assistant in the driver's seat – Meryl opened the van, piled in the canvases and was ready to climb in the passenger side within a matter of minutes.

'Right, we're off,' she said, face flushed from the physical exertion. 'I'm just a phone call away if you need anything. Anything at all. Look after yourself, Gloria.'

With that, Meryl gave Gloria a brief hug before jumping into the passenger seat. Gloria let out a sigh of relief as the van made its way to the end of the long drive, finally disappearing from view as it pulled onto the road. They had done it.

Her reprieve was short-lived, however, as seconds later a very familiar silver Mercedes turned onto the drive and began crawling up towards the house. Greg was home, and there was no chance he hadn't noticed the van.

Gloria took a second to steady herself and wipe the worry from her face. She had managed to convince Greg that all was well so far – surely she could do it for a little longer. She didn't have a choice. Her heart hammered against her chest, but she projected an image of the calm, welcoming housewife as best she could.

'Greg!' she called cheerfully, running up to greet him as he got out of the car, a deep frown already creasing his brow. 'I just got your message about going out for dinner. What's the occasion?'

'What was that van here for?' he asked, clearly not falling for Gloria's attempt at a distraction.

'Oh, that was Meryl Hofmann-Mills. You know, the art dealer?' Greg nodded slowly, his frown unmoved. 'She offered to help me out and put some of my paintings up in her gallery to try and drum up some interest. It might not come to anything, but it's exciting to try, don't you think?'

It took a great deal of effort for Gloria not to continue talking, just to fill the silence, but she knew that would give her away. Instead, she simply smiled at Greg, awaiting his answer.

'That seems like an awful lot of effort for someone who barely knows you,' Greg replied, eyes fixed on Gloria as if probing for weakness.

'Well, you know how persuasive Katie can be!' Gloria laughed, hoping that throwing in Katie's name would put an end to his questions.

'Oh, I should have known she'd be behind this!' He rolled his eyes, but seemed to relax a little. 'Anyway, I'm starving. Why don't you go get changed so we can go out?'

That was close.

CHAPTER FOURTEEN

Four days left.

'I'm sorry, the person you are calling is unavailable.
To leave a message—'

Gloria slammed the phone down on the bed in frustration. Iris still wouldn't speak to her, and there was no way she could explain what was happening through a text message. It was all so complicated, and in all honesty, Gloria wasn't sure Iris would believe her if she did tell her the whole story. She had to tell her something, though. She had to convince Iris to speak to her again and let her know she was coming back to the continent. Picking the phone back up, Gloria typed out a quick message.

> Birthday trip with Greg is off. I'll try my best to get to Amsterdam. Please call me soon. I miss you sweetheart xxx

It was the best she could do for now. Gloria briefly considered calling Elias, but she didn't want Iris to find out she was leaving Greg through him. It wouldn't be right. No, she would just have to keep calling until Iris picked up the phone.

'Teenagers!' Gloria muttered, rubbing her temples.

She already had a headache coming on without this added stress. She hadn't even turned the bedroom light on yet, unsure if she could handle the brightness. Greg had insisted on ordering a third bottle of wine at the restaurant last night, and he'd practically had to carry Gloria to bed by the end of the evening. She'd woken up with her clothes still on and an ache in her back where she'd fallen asleep on top of her handbag.

Which reminds me...

Gloria climbed into the still-crumpled bed sheets and fished out her handbag. She looped the long strap over her head so the bag crossed her body – she didn't want to leave Meryl's money lying around. Gloria had spent most of her life struggling with very little money, and despite the comfort she'd grown used to since marrying Greg, she had never shaken the habit of being protective about cash. When she and Katie had been staying in hostels early on in their friendship, Gloria had been known to carry every penny she had on her person at all times.

Gloria popped open her handbag and stared at the wad of notes within. She still couldn't quite believe her paintings had made her so much money, even if Meryl had perhaps been a little generous with the purchase price. Gloria had sold a few paintings here and there in the past, and her art had supplemented her more tedious part-time jobs in Amsterdam, but having her work on display in a real, professional gallery was like a dream come true.

As she brushed the notes with her fingers, Gloria

remembered Meryl's advice as she'd handed it over.

Don't keep it all in one place, just in case.

She split the bundle in half and walked over to her dresser to stash the money with the catalogue she'd hidden away what felt like forever ago. It seemed as safe a place as any – Greg had never shown an interest in the knick-knacks, makeup and perfume Gloria kept in there.

Gloria pulled open the drawer, and her stomach dropped to her feet.

The catalogue was gone.

Don't panic. Maybe I'm forgetting which drawer I put it in.

She opened every drawer in the dresser, some two or three times as she became increasingly panicked. But it was no use – the catalogue was nowhere to be found. A creeping sense of dread enveloped Gloria's body, and her blood ran cold as she realised what this meant.

He knows.

Gloria's heart pounded in her chest as she stood staring in horror at the empty drawer. She was rooted to the spot, paralysed with fear. When had Greg found it? Gloria was home almost all the time. She'd have noticed him snooping through her drawers. It didn't matter. All that mattered was that he knew.

But *how much* did he know?

Did he know she was going to leave? That she couldn't let him go through with his plans? That in a few days, she'd be out of the country and out of his life forever?

God, I hope not.

Gloria sank down onto the bed and buried her face in her hands, her head spinning. Maybe she should call Katie and ask for her advice. She might be able to join her a few days early, or at the very least, Katie could help her figure out what to do next. She had to clear her had before she called anyone, however; her head was beginning to pound from last night's overindulgence on the wine.

Overindulgence on the wine.

Gloria glanced at the drawer again. Of course she hadn't noticed Greg rooting through her things – she had been unconscious. That snake had got her drunk and put her to bed so he had an opportunity to rummage through her belongings. He'd probably looked at *everything* in there. All of her most private possessions were in that dresser: baby photos of Iris, poems Elias had written for her during their whirlwind romance, journals from her escape across the sea to Europe. The very thought of him rifling through everything that was most private and personal to her turned her stomach.

She had to do something. Sitting and feeling sorry for herself wouldn't resolve the situation. First things first – she had to get rid of this headache.

Gloria quickly stripped out of the previous night's clothes and dragged on a pair of comfortable leggings and a t-shirt, before putting the handbag back over her body. Old habits die hard. She ventured out of the bedroom and into the hallway. The house was silent; she couldn't even hear the birds singing in the garden.

She tiptoed downstairs and into the kitchen, keeping all the lights off, with just the soft light of day creeping in through the windows to guide her. She made a beeline for the medicine drawer where she was certain there must be some paracetamol knocking around. She was usually good at handling hangovers, but this was something else. It was as if all of the stress and pain of the last week was manifesting itself as one of the worst headaches she had ever experienced, gathering behind her eyeballs as if trying to rip her brain from her skull.

She finally fished out an old strip of tablets from the drawer and began to pop them into a trembling hand. She retrieved a glass from the nearest cupboard and padded over to the sink to fill it with water, knowing she was probably dehydrated after drinking nothing but wine for the last half a day.

'We need to talk.'

The sudden sound startled Gloria, and the glass slipped from her unsteady fingers and shattered across the kitchen tiles, showering her bare legs and feet with razor-sharp shards. She stood frozen. A voice in her head screamed for her to run, but she couldn't move. It took all of the strength she could muster to turn around, feet scraping against the surrounding cold shards of glass.

There, stood stone-faced in the doorway, was Greg. And he had the catalogue in his hands.

CHAPTER FIFTEEN

'I-I thought you were at work?'

Gloria just about managed to keep her voice steady. Greg's face was inscrutable, a perfect mask of neutrality. Gloria's eyes flitted to his hands, his pale knuckles betraying him where he was gripping the catalogue.

'I'm working from home today,' he said plainly, as if this was a regular occurrence. 'I thought it would be nice to spend some time with my wife.'

Silence stretched between them as they both waited for the other to address the elephant in the room. Gloria strained to appear calm, though her heart threatened to burst through her chest. Finally, she couldn't bear it any longer.

'That's a very nice thought,' she said quietly, and tore her eyes away from Greg to busy herself tidying up the broken glass still scattered on and around her feet.

'I thought so.'

His cold tone sent a shiver down Gloria's spine as she picked up the largest pieces of glass and placed them one by one on the kitchen counter. She was grateful for the distraction, but she couldn't avoid Greg forever; he was still there, waiting.

'That was careless of you, wasn't it?'

Gloria jumped a little, dropping a piece of glass into the sink. In the tense silence, it seemed to clatter like an alarm bell. 'I didn't expect anyone else to be home,' she answered, forcing herself to turn and face him again. His expression was unchanged and unreadable. 'You startled me.'

There was a painful moment of silence before Greg finally moved, striding forwards to sit at the breakfast bar. He slowly placed the catalogue on the counter and pushed it towards Gloria, one eyebrow raised.

'I see you've discovered my surprise.'

What?

Gloria stood agape as Greg's mouth twisted into a slight smile. He almost looked like he was about to laugh. She tried to speak, to ask him what on Earth he was talking about, but the words caught in her throat.

'I would have preferred to surprise you myself, but it seems like you couldn't keep your sticky fingers out of my study after all.'

Gloria was stunned. Was he really admonishing her for going into his study and discovering his exploitation of her? His smile suggested he might be joking, but the hard glint in his eyes said otherwise.

'I was looking for pencils.' No, she didn't have to explain herself. 'But it doesn't matter why I was there! You owe *me* an explanation, Greg.'

He let out a small laugh, shaking his head. Gloria bristled; how could he be so blasé about this when she felt so violated?

'I wanted to explain it to you myself.' His face softened, and he reached out as if hoping Gloria would take his hand. She didn't move. 'You're the star of the show, Gloria. The crème de la crème! This is a time to celebrate, not sulk.'

Celebrate?

She couldn't believe what she was hearing. Did Greg really think she was *that* stupid?

'What do you mean?' she said slowly, clutching a piece of glass so hard she could feel it cutting into her palm. She had to keep her cool or risk ruining what was left of her plans.

'Why do you think I'm always so keen to show you off? You're special, Gloria, and I wanted to make you finally realise that.'

Gloria swallowed down the bile rising at the back of her throat. A short while ago, she might have believed him. That sickened her more than anything.

'You should have asked me first.' She strained to keep her voice steady and forced herself to maintain eye contact. Greg's smile was fixed in place, but his eyes regarded her with clinical scrutiny, scanning for cracks in her facade. She couldn't crumble now; she had to stay strong.

'I'm sorry, darling. I was doing what I thought was best for you, that's all.'

He stood, and Gloria stiffened, painfully aware of the dusting of glass particles still surrounding her bare feet, preventing escape. She tore her eyes from Greg and busied herself searching for a dustpan in the nearest cupboard, hoping he would leave her alone and end this strange conversation. She reached to feel under the bottom shelf but froze as a cold, firm hand grasped her shoulder. Gloria flinched, but allowed herself to be raised upright.

Greg stood inches away from her, his eyebrows pulled together in a frown. He almost looked worried.

Worried about me.

'I will look after you, Gloria,' he said quietly, searching

eyes scanning her face before settling on her own. 'This is all for you. For *us.*'

He brushed a strand of hair from Gloria's face, and her skin crawled at his touch. She fought to keep her face calm, though every fibre of her being was desperate to sever contact. She had to stay strong, to stick to the plan. Greg knew she had discovered his secret, but that was it. She could still get out, as long as she kept playing the loyal wife.

'I still think you should have told me.' Gloria managed to paint a small smile across her face. 'But I suppose it is a little bit exciting.'

Greg's grin widened.

He thinks he's got me.

'Exactly, darling! All the girls at work are jealous.' He grabbed Gloria's waist and lifted her safely over the glass. 'You just relax your pretty little head, carry on painting your pictures and let me worry about all this, okay?'

She wanted to shout, to scream and punch and kick, but she couldn't. She had to hold out for a little longer. Fighting every urge in her body, she put a hand on Greg's arm and adopted her most innocent smile.

'Okay, darling.'

CHAPTER SIXTEEN

This is exhausting.

Feigning normality was proving more difficult than Gloria had expected, especially with Greg stalking her all day like an unwelcome shadow. He typically spent his working from home days holed up in his office, oblivious to her existence, but today was an exception. She found him lurking in every room she entered, keeping a watchful eye under the guise of wanting to spend time with her. That big house had never felt so small.

Gloria managed to find some semblance of peace sitting at the breakfast bar with the patio doors wide open, letting in a soft summer breeze that caressed her bare arms. She absent-mindedly doodled rough landscapes in one of her old sketchpads while mentally drawing up a list of things she needed to pack for Paris.

'I thought you might have wanted to go to your studio.'

Greg sat at the opposite end of the counter, narrow eyes peering over the top of his laptop. Gloria had no doubt he spent as much time studying her as he did the reports on his screen.

'I'm still feeling a bit delicate after last night.' Technically, she wasn't lying.

In truth, Gloria yearned to paint, to lose herself in her art and shut out the rest of the world, but she didn't want Greg following her into her studio. She couldn't find sanctuary with him breathing down her neck, and didn't want him to realise quite how many paintings Meryl had taken back to the gallery.

'Oh really?' Greg said, closing his laptop and raising an eyebrow. 'I'd have thought you'd have developed a high tolerance to alcohol by now.'

'Yes, well...it turns out three bottles in one night is too much even for me.'

She tried to go back to her drawing, to project an image of indifference, but she couldn't prevent the question that had been rattling around in her head all day from bubbling up and tumbling out of her mouth.

'So...do you think you'll work from home tomorrow as well?'

Gloria had carefully laid out plans for her final days before leaving for good. Plans that did not involve Greg being home all the time. She didn't like the short, sharp laugh which answered her. She looked up to see him smirking at her, sharp brown eyes glittering with malevolence.

'That's the best part, darling. The lab team have managed to get their sample kits ready earlier than expected. Tomorrow, I'll be going in to pick them up, and then we can immortalise you forever. Isn't that great?'

Gloria's blood turned to ice. She fought to keep her face still, pinching her lips to hold back the scream threatening to burst from her throat. Greg was watching her, eyebrows raised in anticipation, eagle eyes scanning her face, ready to study her reaction.

'Oh, is that how it works?' She cringed at the weakness of her reply, but it was all she could come up with under the weight of Greg's stare. 'I thought there might be some sort of procedure or something.'

Greg let out another small laugh. 'Things have advanced a little since your Biology GCSE, Gloria.'

She narrowed her eyes at him, cracks starting to form in her veneer.

Breathe. Don't react.

'I'm not as stupid as you might think, dear.' She managed to force a small smile. 'I'm sure you could dumb it down to explain it for me. I'm not just a pretty face!'

Greg rolled his eyes a little, but humoured her. Arrogance always won out with Greg – he had always loved the sound of his own voice. 'It's a lot simpler and more cost-effective than it used to be. With one small kit, I can gather several viable samples – skin, hair, saliva, blood – and as long as I keep them chilled, they can be in the lab the following day for the first round of implants. If those aren't successful, we might have to try other procedures, but hopefully that won't be necessary.'

Wait.

'What does it mean if they aren't successful?' She wasn't sure if she wanted to know, but she couldn't stop herself from asking the question.

'We dispose of the embryos and start again.' Greg shrugged. 'Oh, don't look so aghast, Gloria, it's just business.'

She felt sick. Any remaining composure fell away from her features, replaced by pure revulsion. How could this man, who she had once loved, speak so casually about something so monstrous?

I can't do this.

Her heart pounded in her chest as she rose from her

stool, pale hands gripping the cool marble to steady herself. She couldn't listen to this anymore.

'I'm feeling unwell again,' she said feebly, no longer caring how believable she was. 'I'm going to go for a lie down.'

Gloria was vaguely aware of Greg's dark chuckle as she stumbled past him into the hallway and to the downstairs toilet. She just had time to reach the bowl before throwing up the meagre contents of her stomach.

◆——— · ● ◆ ● · ——— ◆

It was after midnight when Greg came upstairs. Gloria had been in bed for hours, using the excuse of hangover recovery, but she hadn't slept. How could she, knowing her husband was downstairs plotting to harvest her body in only one day's time? Instead, she hid under the covers, eyes wide and heart hammering, knowing this would be her final night in the house. There was no other choice.

Gloria stiffened as the door swung open, bathing the bedroom in stark, white light. Her heart raced, but she fought to keep her breathing steady, eyes clenched shut. She didn't want to speak to Greg; she didn't even want to acknowledge his existence. Following their conversation today, she was at breaking point. She couldn't keep up the charade any longer.

Gloria's entire body tensed as she felt Greg's weight drop down on the other side of the king-sized bed, but she didn't move. She forced herself to breathe through trembling lips, hoping Greg would assume she was asleep and leave her alone. Her stomach turned as the weight of his arm settled over her torso, and he pulled her body towards his own.

Silent tears threatened to creep from behind Gloria's closed eyelids as she felt Greg's hot, heavy breathing on the back of her neck. Still, she didn't move, lying perfectly still as the seconds dragged on for what seemed like an eternity. It was to her immense relief when Greg's arm went limp, and his breathing slowed as sleep finally took him. The taste of salt tingled on her tongue as she released a quiet sob.

She just needed to get through this one night, and then she could leave. Forever.

There was no way she would be able to fall asleep.

CHAPTER SEVENTEEN

Gloria jumped out of bed as soon as Greg was out the door. Her body ached all over from lack of sleep, but it didn't matter; she had to go.

She ran over to Greg's wardrobe, pulled out his leather travel bag and threw it onto the bed, frantically tearing clothes out of her own wardrobe and stuffing them inside. In her frenzy, she didn't take note of what she was packing; she just knew she needed clothes. Before long, she was throwing in makeup, perfume, photos, anything she could think of which she might need once she was out of the house.

This isn't how it was supposed to happen, she thought bitterly. She should have had a couple more days to properly plan and pack. She'd even planned to write a scathing farewell note to Greg, letting him know exactly what she thought of him. Now all she could hope for was to be far away from this house before he returned from work and realised she was gone. She'd worry about how she was going to actually achieve that on her journey into the city. The train ride would give her time to think. Now, she just needed to get out.

Once Gloria had crammed as many items into the bag as could be reasonably expected to fit, she forced the zip closed and retrieved her handbag from under her pillow, looping the long strap over her body so it rested on her hip. She checked her passport and money were still there – they were too precious to risk keeping anywhere else while Greg was still sniffing around. Cursing herself, she scraped her dead phone from the dresser and threw it in. With Greg's constant surveillance yesterday, she had completely forgotten to charge it.

Hitching the travel bag onto her shoulder, she headed for the door and took a final moment to look back at the bedroom that had imprisoned her in recent years. She had spent her time in this house feeling trapped and suffocated but had never been able to figure out why. At times, she'd convinced herself it was homesickness for Amsterdam and the buzz of the city, told herself it would pass. It never had, though, and she was now certain it never would have. She didn't belong here, and she never had.

As she hurriedly made her way down the wide staircase to the hallway, a new sensation began bubbling up in Gloria's stomach: she was excited. Excited to be free. Free from Greg, free from this God-forsaken house, free from living on eggshells as she endlessly tried to be someone she wasn't. For the first time in years, Gloria was truly hopeful, and it felt good. She unhooked her coat from the stand by the front door and grabbed one of Greg's expensive black umbrellas. She thought she could hear rain outside.

See you in Hell, she thought with a smirk, pulling at the doorknob.

The door didn't move. Gloria scrambled in her bag for her keys and jammed one into the lock, but it wouldn't fit. She stared at it in the palm of her hand, confused. This was the key she had used since the day she moved in with Greg –

it had to fit. She thrust the key into the lock again, but again it wouldn't go in. Gloria's chest tightened as she realised what this must mean.

He's changed the locks.

Her heart pounded, but she took a deep breath, trying to force herself to remain calm. There were other ways out. She ran through the kitchen to the back door and tried her other key, but it was no use – she was trapped. As panic gripped her, she raced to the kitchen window and pushed at the handle, but it wouldn't budge. The window key, usually thrown haphazardly on the windowsill, was gone. She was sealed in.

Gloria's chest ached as she forced air through her constricting lungs. Stood in the stark, cavernous kitchen and staring out through the glass door at the lush, verdant garden, she felt like a trapped animal, unwillingly confined to captivity. She had to breathe, to think. She had spent almost every day alone in this house for over a decade. If anyone could find a way out, it was her.

Biting her lip, she paced the kitchen, circling the breakfast bar in an attempt to slow her racing mind.

Think. Think. Think.

Greg had locked the obvious escape routes, but that didn't mean there was no way out – he thought Gloria was clueless, after all. She stopped pacing and scanned the room. When not eating or drinking, the only time she came through here was to use the downstairs toilet when painting in her studio.

The toilet.

Gloria went into the small room most days. Located just off the kitchen, it meant minimal disruption to her creative flow. Most importantly, she knew for a fact there was a window in there. A window she opened wide in the warm summer months to stop it from getting too stuffy. It wouldn't be easy, but she was almost sure she could fit through it. She would have to. It was her only option.

She strode across the room and around the corner to the unassuming, narrow white door. It blended in with the crisp wallpaper so well that most visitors didn't even notice it was there – apparently, the wealthy don't like to acknowledge their bodily functions.

She pushed the door open and slipped into the room. With the travel bag slung over her shoulder, she could only just fit in the compact space. Greg's lack of interest in the room was evident everywhere, from the mismatched fittings to the garish floral wallpaper. He hadn't bothered to put his stamp on it when he bought the house, content to keep it hidden from public view. Gloria, however, adored the quirkiness of the place. It had character. Aside from her studio, it was probably the only thing she would miss about the house.

Goosebumps prickled Gloria's skin as she reached over the sink for the window. This was her best chance. If this was also locked, she was trapped, like a bird in a cage, able to see her freedom but with no way of reaching it. Her breath caught as the handle turned and the window eased back an inch, and she choked back a sob of relief.

Thank God.

She dropped the travel bag on the floor and slammed both her palms into the window, sending it swinging out towards the garden. It would be a tight squeeze, but she was sure she could wriggle through. It might be an unpleasant drop onto the paving stones, but she didn't care; she was getting out of this house.

Gloria lifted the travel bag and pushed it out into the garden, flinching as it crashed into a pot of tulips. She twisted her handbag onto her back and clambered up onto the sink. This wasn't going to be a graceful manoeuvre. She lowered her body and edged forwards towards freedom, but froze as a cold, low voice pierced the air.

'Going somewhere?'

Gloria's stomach turned to ice as she looked over her shoulder to see Greg, eyes ablaze.

CHAPTER EIGHTEEN

Gloria's throat dried up; she couldn't say anything. She remained still, crouched absurdly on the sink, staring into Greg's eyes. They burned with molten fury, yet the rest of his face was eerily calm. Her heartbeat roared in her ears as her fight or flight response engaged, adrenaline coursing through her body. Greg started to slowly make his way towards her, and she seized her moment, launching herself through the window. She had barely taken a single breath of fresh air when rough hands grabbed her waist from behind and pulled her back.

She kicked and struggled as Greg dragged her out into the hallway. He threw her onto the stairs like a rag doll, and a sharp pain shot up her spine as her back made contact with the corner of the bottom step.

'You're not going anywhere,' he snarled.

Gloria started to lift herself off the stairs to sprint for the door, still ajar following Greg's quiet entrance, but he was too quick, grabbing her arm and beginning to drag her up the stairs. Gloria clawed at his hand, trying in vain to pry his fingers from her flesh, but he had an iron grip that could not be dislodged. Panic gripped her, and she thrashed and pulled away from him, not caring if she might end up throwing herself down the stairs.

Greg was stronger than Gloria had expected and didn't flinch as he continued to pull her, tightening his grasp until it was painful. She began punching his hand and arm, desperate to loosen his grip.

'You're hurting me!' she shrieked, landing more blows on his arm, but to no avail.

Greg didn't listen. He proceeded to pull Gloria up the stairs, deaf to her shouts of pain as she tripped and scraped her shins on the stair edges.

'You're...you're a monster!' she screamed, fighting back tears as they reached the landing. Greg was unmoved, and simply continued marching onwards until he reached the guest bedroom.

'A monster?' He pulled her close, grabbing her face and squeezing hard until Gloria was sure she could feel the inside of her cheeks slicing open against her teeth. 'And what does that make you?'

He released her with such force she would have fallen to the floor, had she not still been locked in his vice-like grip.

'I'm your wife!' she choked between sobs, unable to hold back the tears any longer. 'I loved you!'

Greg barked a cruel laugh. 'Now, let's be honest, dear. You never loved me. You loved my money. You loved the lifestyle I could offer, and you loved that I paid for everything, even your brat of a daughter. That's it.'

"That's not true!' Gloria sobbed, tugging away from him with such force her shoulder felt on the verge of dislocation.

'Would you have even cared if it wasn't your DNA I was using? If it was some other man or woman being used to keep you in the lap of luxury?' Greg asked, his voice cold and unfeeling, his eyes boring into hers.

'Of course I would have!' Gloria spat back at him. 'I thought you were saving lives. This...this is eugenics!'

Greg's malevolent smile turned Gloria's blood cold. 'I told you yesterday, darling. It's just business. That's all.'

He dragged her helplessly through the doorway into the bedroom and threw her roughly across the room. A new wave of pain shot up her back as she collided with the hard wooden floor. Fighting back wasn't working – she had to try something else. She crawled meekly to the bed and dragged herself upright, holding on to the bedpost for support.

'You might as well make yourself comfortable because you're going to be seeing a lot of these four walls. You clearly can't be trusted to have free roam of the house.'

She didn't say anything. She didn't even look up at him. She rubbed her eyes to try and stem the flow of silent tears still pouring from them, and bit her lip to force herself to stay silent. Greg took a few slow steps towards her.

'Look, you'll come around and see this is for the best, I'm sure of it.' He stepped even closer, and in her peripheral vision, Gloria thought she saw him reach out for her. 'I'm right, Gloria. Once you—'

She gave him no time to finish his sentence. Instead, Gloria grabbed his arms and used all of the strength she could muster to drive her knee into his crotch. Greg's eyes bulged, whether in shock or pain, she couldn't tell. He staggered back, bending over in agony, and Gloria took her chance. She rushed out onto the landing and almost lost her footing as she careered down the stairs. The hallway was a blur as she wrenched open the front door and sprinted down the driveway.

Through the haze of tears, Gloria had no idea where was going. She was at the mercy of her pounding feet as she took random turns left and right, up tree-lined streets and down shaded snickets. Her lungs were on fire and she was vaguely aware that it was raining, but she didn't stop. She had to get away, to make sure Greg couldn't follow. Her heartbeat roared in her ears. A stabbing pain in her side begged her to stop, but she barrelled forwards, terror driving her footsteps. She stumbled onwards until it became impossible to take a breath, and finally slumped onto a nearby garden wall, gasping for air. She put her head between her legs, retching from the sudden expenditure of effort.

When she finally lifted her head up, Gloria took a moment to survey her surroundings, and quickly realised she had no idea where she was. She had stopped in what seemed like a pleasant suburban street. It was lined with large, detached terracotta-coloured houses, each one set back from the road and sporting a lush, well-landscaped front garden. She knew she had to get to the train station, to get out and into the city as soon as she could, but in her distress she had paid no attention to the direction she was running in. She couldn't begin to guess which way she needed to go. Now she was stationary, she became aware of how hard it was raining. She was already soaked through. She needed to get help – and out of the rain.

She rose from the wall on unsteady legs and walked up the street, examining each house as she passed. It was clearly an affluent area, and although Gloria knew she was being paranoid, she was wracked with fear that one of Greg's friends, colleagues or even clients could be behind one of these doors and would recognise her. It was ridiculous, she knew, but she couldn't risk Greg being alerted to her presence, not after what happened at the house.

As she continued up the street, arms wrapped around her body for warmth, one house stood out. It had a large, seven-seater car sitting on the driveway, and the trampoline peeking over the fence from the back garden suggested the presence of children. A family lived here. Her gut told her these people were not linked to Greg, and she hoped beyond hope that they would help her.

She walked slowly to the front door and tried to smarten up her bedraggled appearance, smoothing her damp hair behind her ears before ringing the doorbell. A tall, dark-haired woman answered, perhaps a few years younger than Gloria, and she looked her up and down, confused.

'Can I help you?' she asked slowly, clearly unsure what to expect from the soaking wet visitor standing on her doorstep.

'I really hope so,' Gloria began, taking care to appear calm so as not to unsettle the woman. 'I'm terribly lost, and my phone's out of battery. I know this is unusual, and I don't mean to impose, but could I possibly come in and borrow your phone to order a taxi to the train station? I promise I'll be in and out in no time. Please.'

The woman glanced back over her shoulder into the house and seemed reluctant to let this stranger into her home. She hesitated a moment more before finally nodding and stepping back to let Gloria into the hallway. She hadn't realised how cold she was until the warmth of the house washed over her. It felt like a blessing.

'Thank you so much, um...'

'Sarah,' the woman replied with a small, sympathetic smile. 'You must be freezing. Here, sit in the living room and warm up while I get you a towel to dry yourself off a bit.'

Gloria smiled gratefully, following Sarah through to a

spacious, modern living room at the front of the house and sinking down into a plush, grey armchair. After her frantic escape, the soft cushions were blissfully comfortable, and she took the opportunity to put everything out of her mind for a moment and enjoy the peace, if only for a short while.

'Who are you?'

A small voice startled Gloria, and she opened her eyes to see a young boy stood on the rug in front of her. He was perhaps six or seven years old, with a mop of messy, dark brown hair and a few smudges on his cheek suggesting he had been playing with paints. He looked up at Gloria with large, expectant eyes.

'My name's Gloria,' she answered, and held out a hand to him. He hesitated briefly, but took her hand and shook it briskly. 'What's your name?'

'Daniel,' he said simply, a look of concern creasing his forehead. 'Are you okay? You look scared.'

Gloria couldn't help but smile at the boy. He had that same look of curiosity and habit for asking lots of questions that Iris had at his age.

'I'm lost,' she answered carefully, not wanting to share any of the hurtful truth with an innocent child, 'so I suppose I am little bit scared. Your mummy is going to help me, though, so don't worry.'

That seemed to reassure Daniel, and a smile started to creep across his small face. 'I want to help you, too.'

He wandered over to a large toy box in the corner of the room and began rummaging around inside. Gloria watched him curiously – how could this little boy possibly help her? Daniel came back a few minutes later, proudly holding out a small stuffed dinosaur no bigger than Gloria's palm. He reached out, took her hand and placed the dinosaur into it.

'This is Rexy,' he explained proudly. 'When I was scared, Mum used to give him to me so I'd feel brave. I don't need him anymore, so you should take him, so you won't be scared when you're lost.'

The young boy looked so pleased with himself, and Gloria felt tears return to her eyes from this small act of kindness.

'Wow, that's very, very nice of you. But I'm not sure your mummy would be happy about—'

'Take it.' Gloria turned her head to see Sarah standing in the doorway, smiling warmly at her son.

Gloria nodded, closed her fingers around the small dinosaur and held it to her chest.

'I feel braver already,' she said, and Daniel beamed back at her, his eyes sparkling.

'Now,' Sarah said, walking to the centre of the room and bending down to speak to Daniel, 'why don't you go and fetch our visitor some cookies from the kitchen while she dries off?'

Daniel nodded enthusiastically and ran out of the room, leaving the two women alone.

'He's a lovely boy,' Gloria said.

'Thank you. He can be a handful, but he's a really good kid.' Sarah smiled warmly and handed Gloria a large white towel. 'Here, you dry yourself off, and I'll go order you a taxi to the station.'

Sarah left the room, and Gloria made the most of the towel she'd been offered, drying off her hair and soaking up as much of the moisture from her clothes as she could manage. Despite it being the middle of summer, it was a cool day, and Gloria wasn't relishing the idea of going back outside in damp clothes.

Daniel soon returned with a plate full of chocolate chip

cookies, a smear of chocolate around his mouth suggesting he'd tried one or two on his way back from the kitchen. He held out the plate to Gloria, who took a cookie gratefully, only now realising that she hadn't eaten all day.

'Mum says she's ringing for a taxi,' Daniel said through a mouthful of cookie crumbs. 'Are you going home?'

Gloria glanced up at the window, rain lashing against the pane.

'No,' she said sadly. 'No, I can't go home.'

CHAPTER NINETEEN

The jarring sound of an obnoxiously loud announcement crackling through the tannoy system roused Gloria from her uneasy sleep. She had been so exhausted as she settled down into her seat on the train that she'd fallen asleep within minutes, curled up against the cold, grimy window. In her dazed state, she didn't register what the announcer was saying, but the sight of the red and white sign through the window told her she had arrived in Waterloo.

Stepping off the train onto the chilly platform, Gloria felt grateful for the hooded jacket Sarah had given her for the journey, and she pulled the zip up to her chin to try and keep out the worst of the cold. Sarah had refused to accept any money for it, insisting it was old anyway, and her husband wouldn't miss it. Gloria smiled as she walked briskly through the station – she really had been lucky to knock on that door. She tried to make a mental note of the address so she could send them something once she was finally settled somewhere far away from here, to at least try and pay them back for their kindness.

Thankfully, the station was relatively quiet, with only a few tourists milling about the platforms, so it didn't take long for Gloria to find a vacant black cab at the taxi rank. The driver was a surly bald man sporting a flat cap and a scowl.

'Where to?' he grunted as Gloria climbed into the cab and fastened her seatbelt.

'Can you take me here?' she asked, holding up Meryl's business card bearing the gallery's address. The driver nodded silently and pulled away into the busy London streets.

Nervous butterflies fluttered in Gloria's stomach. With her phone dead, she'd had no chance to warn Meryl of her arrival, and she was unsure how welcome she would be when she turned up unannounced, sopping wet and carrying nothing more than the clothes on her back and the handbag she'd luckily been wearing before Greg's attack. This was assuming Meryl was even at the gallery; there was every chance it was closed, and then Gloria wouldn't know what to do next. But she couldn't worry about that now. One step at a time.

The windows were fogged up from the rain and, without her phone to guide her, Gloria was completely at the mercy of the driver as they snaked their way through Central London. With only the sound of the cab creeping along the city streets to distract her, Gloria's mind wandered. She couldn't help but wonder what Greg was doing now. Had he gone looking for her when she ran out? Would he accept she was gone and let it be? A twist in her gut told her that was impossible, that it wasn't over yet, but she hoped she had put enough distance between them to escape his grasp, at least.

Gloria did feel a small sliver of satisfaction as she imagined Greg returning to work tomorrow morning to tell them the plan was off; they couldn't create copies of his wife after all. She briefly hoped he would be in big trouble for his failure, that they'd sack him from the firm altogether, that he'd lose everything, just as she had. But despite everything, the callous thought stirred a twinge of guilt in her stomach. She *had* loved him, no matter what he said.

'Just up here on the left.'

The driver's gruff voice broke Gloria out of her stupor, and she snapped back to attention as the cab rolled to a stop. She glanced at the meter, handed over a note from her handbag and told the driver to keep the change. The resulting grunt sounded almost appreciative. Gloria thanked her lucky stars she had kept all of her cash on her person, just like she had in the old days. She'd have nothing, otherwise, and no chance of surviving without Greg. Some old habits didn't need breaking, after all.

Gloria drew her hood up and stepped out into the rain, bracing herself against the chill of the dwindling afternoon. The cab sped away behind her, leaving her alone, standing in the street looking up at the magnificent Hoffman-Mills Gallery, awestruck. Unlike the drab, everyday buildings to either side of it, the gallery was a riot of colour, with sweeping arcs and geometric shapes of all hues and shades. Despite the multitude of colours and patterns, nothing clashed. The abstract forms melded together perfectly, creating a kaleidoscope of beauty right in the midst of an otherwise typical London street. The grey skies and driving rain only enhanced the vividness of the place, haloing it as a haven of culture in an otherwise stark environment.

Gloria's eyes scanned the row of circular windows facing out onto the bustling street, and she shuddered with relief – the lights were on. Meryl was still in. Bracing herself for an awkward conversation, she took a deep breath and pushed open the sleek glass doors leading inside.

The interior of the gallery was a great contrast to the outside of the building. Where outside there had been a mad array of vibrant colour, inside there was a subtle, simple style reminiscent of Meryl herself. The spacious, open-plan reception area was bathed in warm hues of beige, amber and gold, which were at once beautiful and comforting. Through open doorways to the front and side of the room, Gloria could see the beginnings of various art exhibitions, and for a brief moment, she wondered where Meryl planned on displaying her work.

'Can I help you?'

The sudden voice surprised Gloria, and she became aware of a tall, well-dressed man standing by a small reception desk to her right. His wrinkled nose suggested he was not impressed by Gloria's sudden arrival, and she became painfully aware of her unkempt appearance.

'Yes, I hope so.' Gloria tried her best to sound like she belonged in the gallery, despite being dressed in dungarees and an oversized men's jacket, dripping rainwater over the polished tiled floor. 'I need to see Meryl. It's quite urgent.'

The man raised an eyebrow, and his eyes scanned Gloria up and down with all the subtlety of a freight train. 'Ms Hofmann-Mills is not on site today, I am afraid. You will have to make an appointment for another time.'

'No, you don't understand.' Gloria approached the desk and looked up at the man, hoping to garner his sympathy. 'I'm a friend of Meryl's and I really need her help. If you could just call her and tell her I'm here, she—'

'Ms Hoffman-Mills already donates to many charitable causes,' the man broke in, speaking a little louder to override the end of Gloria's plea. 'I'm afraid we're not in a position to support unsolicited requests for aid. If you need urgent shelter or support, I suggest you go through the proper channels.'

Wait, does this guy think I'm homeless?

'You don't understand!' Panic began rising inside her, and Gloria gripped tightly on to the reception desk. 'Meryl knows me. Please, if you could just—'

'Gloria?'

She spun around to see an unfamiliar man approaching her from the entrance to the nearest exhibition. He was younger than her, perhaps in his late twenties, with dark skin, kind brown eyes and a warm smile. He looked at Gloria with an expression of immediate recognition, but she was certain she had never seen this man before.

'I'm sorry,' she said, uncomfortably aware the receptionist was listening to every word. 'Have we met before?'

'Of course!' He smacked himself in the forehead. 'Sorry, sorry! I'm Samuel, Meryl's assistant. I was driving the van when we collected your paintings. I guess you couldn't see me, but I saw you through the mirrors and recognised you. I hope I didn't startle you.'

Gloria's knees almost buckled with relief. 'No, not at all. It's good to finally meet you.'

She glanced over her shoulder at the receptionist and pulled Samuel by the arm to a more private spot away from the doorway. 'I don't know how much Meryl told you, but I'm in trouble and I need to see her. Do you know where she is?'

Samuel's eyebrows knotted together as a concerned frown creased his face. 'She's out meeting a buyer at the moment. But, hey! My shift is almost over – why don't we grab something to eat while she's gone and I'll try to take your mind off it until she gets home?'

Gloria smiled and placed a grateful hand on Samuel's arm. 'That sounds wonderful.'

CHAPTER TWENTY

'That was delicious.' Gloria said through the last mouthful of burrito, wiping her guacamole-covered hands on a napkin. 'I've never eaten here before.'

'I know it's probably a bit more basic than places you're used to eating at.' Samuel smiled, looking a little embarrassed. 'But I love it.'

Gloria surveyed the bustling little Mexican diner they'd taken shelter in. It was small, with all the customers sharing one long, communal table, but it was also wonderfully colourful and full of life. Excitable chit chat filled the air as families, friends and lovers shared a simple, wholesome meal. It was a world away from the formal, high-end restaurants Greg had always insisted they dined at. Samuel came here often, it seemed, as the young woman behind the counter knew his order already and the meal he'd recommended for Gloria had been an excellent choice.

'I love it, too.' She beamed, meeting Samuel's eyes with a reassuring smile. 'I take it you're a regular?'

Samuel gave a small, shy shrug, but Gloria thought she caught him sneaking a glance back at the girl behind the counter. 'I love Mexican food, and this place is so...cosy, you know?'

Gloria couldn't help but let out a small laugh. 'Yeah, I

know.' She picked at her nails awkwardly, aware of the silence which had descended between them. 'When did you say Meryl would be home?'

Samuel glanced down at his watch. 'Any time now, really. I left her a message to call me when she's finished her meeting, so it's imminent. In the meantime...would it help at all to talk about what happened?'

Gloria blinked. She hadn't expected to have to explain her situation yet, and Samuel's directness caught her off guard.

'No, no, don't worry! You don't have to tell me. Sorry, it was rude of me to ask,' he said, seeming embarrassed by Gloria's hesitance.

'It's okay.' Gloria sighed. Samuel had been so kind to her since she'd turned up, she owed him some explanation, at least, even if it wasn't the full story. 'My husband found out I was trying to leave, and he...he tried to stop me.'

Samuel's eyes widened, clearly (and correctly) assuming that Greg hadn't been gentle in his efforts to prevent her from leaving. 'Oh, I'm sorry, Gloria. I hope he didn't...well, I hope you're okay.'

She squirmed a little under Samuel's caring gaze. She wasn't used to such immediate and earnest sympathy, and didn't really know how to respond. Thankfully, they were soon interrupted by a loud, cheerful ringtone erupting from Samuel's phone, and he jumped up to take the call.

Gloria fiddled anxiously with her napkin while Samuel stood outside talking to Meryl. From her seat at the table, it was impossible to guess how the conversation was going. Samuel was gesturing with his hands, but whether it was in a positive or negative way, she couldn't tell. Gloria's stomach fluttered with nervous anticipation. She had come to the city assuming Meryl would take her in during her hour of need, but what if she was wrong? What if buying the paintings was as far as her new friend's generosity would stretch? After all, they'd only known each other a couple of weeks. Gloria's chest tightened and she began to feel very foolish. For all she knew, Meryl and Samuel were discussing her audacity right now, wondering how best to deal with her without seeming callous.

A lifetime seemed to pass before Samuel returned, though in reality it couldn't have been more than ten minutes. Gloria had torn her napkin to shreds during the wait, and hurried to hide it under her plate before Samuel sat down across from her again. He placed his phone on the table and regarded Gloria with an unreadable expression on his face.

'Meryl's home.' Samuel smiled, and Gloria's anxiety melted away as she looked into his kind brown eyes. 'Let's go!'

◆———•●◆●•———◆

Gloria snuggled deeper into the wingback armchair, cradling her cup of cocoa tightly so the warmth could spread through her body. After spending the day in the brisk London air, drenched to the bone, she was grateful for the opportunity to thaw her numb body.

Meryl's apartment was more traditional than she had expected, tastefully decorated with an eclectic mix of antiques and plush, patterned rugs. Gloria wiggled her bare toes to enjoy the comfort of the thick, luxurious shag pile beneath her feet. She felt more at home here than she had for years in her own house, and that realisation saddened her. How many years had she wasted trying to convince herself she was happy with Greg, just for him to betray her? The thought made her feel hollow.

'Are you feeling better, dear?' Meryl appeared in the doorway to the living room with a bundle of towels tucked under one arm. 'Samuel has gone home, but he'll be back in the morning with a few supplies for you. Don't worry, I gave him a list so he won't be left to his own devices!'

'Much better. Thank you so much, Meryl.' Gloria smiled up at the older woman, a swell of gratitude rising in her chest. 'I don't know what I did to deserve your kindness.'

Meryl walked over and sat on the sofa across from Gloria's chair. It was a beautiful mustard-coloured Chesterfield; Meryl really did have exquisite taste. 'You're a good person, Gloria, you deserve to feel safe and happy. Sometimes I think you forget that.'

Gloria looked away, unsure how to respond. She wasn't used to receiving compliments, especially not ones about her character, and she had never really learned how to deal with them.

'Now,' Meryl continued, choosing to ignore Gloria's awkwardness, 'I've brought you some towels so you can have a hot bath and warm up, and a fresh pair of my pyjamas for you to sleep in. They'll probably hang off your slender figure, but at least they'll be comfy!'

Gloria giggled, but cut her laughter short as she noticed a look of concern creep into Meryl's face. Her eyes locked onto Gloria's and her light-hearted tone dissolved into something more serious. 'Before you go anywhere...why don't you tell me what happened?'

Gloria hesitated.

Just tell her. Tell her everything.

Before she could stop herself, Gloria was giving Meryl a blow by blow account of the entire ordeal. Meryl's eyes widened with horror as the words spilled from Gloria's mouth, each sentence revealing a terrible new truth. What Gloria had discovered in Greg's office, the photo of Victoria, his assault on her when she'd tried to leave – everything.

Once she had finished, a silence fell across the room. Meryl stood slowly and walked over to Gloria, pulling her gently out of the chair. She enveloped her in a tight embrace, murmuring softly into her mass of red curls.

'You're safe now.'

Gloria wished she could believe her words. Even here, wrapped in the warmth of her friend's comforting arms, miles away from the dangerous man she now despised, a tight ball of doubt in her stomach told her it wasn't over yet.

CHAPTER TWENTY-ONE

Gloria awoke to the sound of rushing London morning traffic vibrating through the sash windows of Meryl's spare bedroom. Her ears had become accustomed to the serene silence of leafy rural Surrey, where the hustle and bustle of inner city life was a distant memory of a misspent youth. It felt good for the world around her to be full of life again, to be part of something big and vibrant, rather than stuck in her own bubble of perpetual solitude. She pulled a blanket around her shoulders and stepped out of the warm, comfortable bed to pull back the curtains and examine the scene below.

The roads were packed with cars, taxis, bicycles and buses, all fighting for pole position in the narrow inner-city roads, and Gloria realised she had no idea what time it was. Back at home, the busy traffic would suggest she had awoken in the middle of the morning rush hour, but here it could be any time of day – the city was always teeming with life. Her eyes scanned the London skyline, taking in the mix of lavish and ordinary buildings, big and small, old and new. The sky itself was painted a bright pale grey, with a hint of sunshine glistening behind a veil of thin cloud. A fresh morning for a fresh start.

But what now?

With her original plan thrown into chaos, Gloria needed

to rethink her next steps. Katie wasn't expecting her for a few more days, but getting her up to speed would be a sensible starting point. Then they could work together on a new plan. Gloria wondered if Katie would even believe what had happened. She had never been Greg's biggest fan and had never pretended otherwise, but would she ever have thought he was capable of all this? Gloria could hardly believe it herself. It all felt like a horrible dream she wished she could wake up from.

Creeping to the bedroom door, Gloria eased it open and slipped through, moving as quietly as she could to avoid disturbing Meryl. She had been so exhausted after her bath the night before, she'd gone straight to bed and collapsed into a deep sleep, leaving what meagre belongings she'd been able to bring with her back in the living room. As she tiptoed across the narrow hallway and into the living room, she glanced at the ornate metal clock hung above the fireplace: it was already nine o'clock.

Have I really slept for that long?

She must have been more exhausted than she realised and, in truth, she felt infinitely better for having a decent rest. Sneaking up to the armchair where she'd left her handbag, she quietly opened it to take out her phone.

It was gone.

Frowning, Gloria lifted the chair cushions and ran her hand down every crease, fingers grasping desperately for the lost device. It must have fallen out of her bag when she got up. Or maybe she had taken it out and it had slid off the chair during the night. Either way, it *had* to be there, somewhere.

It was no use, however. The phone was nowhere to be found. Her chest tightened and her heart began to race. If she had lost her phone, she'd lost her link with Katie, her ability to communicate with Iris, everything. Desperation gripped her, and she dropped to her knees, hands scrambling under the armchair, the sofa, anywhere her phone might have ended up during the night.

'Oh, dear, don't – you might find something embarrassing!'

Gloria jumped, startled, banging her head against the base of the wingback chair. She emerged from under the furniture to see a smiling Meryl standing in the doorway, leaning against the doorframe in a beautifully patterned silk dressing gown. Gloria turned and sat down on the rug in the middle of the room, her hand pressed against the dull ache in her skull.

'Sorry, Meryl, I wasn't prying,' she said through gritted teeth. She had hit her head harder than she thought. 'I'm worried I might have lost my phone. It should be around here somewhere.'

'Ah.' Meryl held up a finger and walked back out of the room, leaving Gloria sat puzzled on the floor, still clutching her aching head. When Meryl returned, a familiar device dangled from her fingers and Gloria beamed with delight.

'Oh, thank God! Where was it?'

'It fell out of your bag last night when you left for your bath, and I noticed it was dead, so I left it charging overnight for you.' She walked over and handed the phone to Gloria. 'I've heard it go off a couple of times this morning already, so you might want to check who's been trying to get hold of you.'

Meryl's eyes were sympathetic. They both knew who might have been contacting her.

Gloria hesitated before standing up and taking the phone, not sure if she wanted to see for herself. Up until now, she'd been blissfully ignorant, enjoying Meryl's company and a change of surroundings to somewhere altogether more pleasant than her own house. A cold knot in her stomach began to form as she unlocked the phone to finally face reality. Most of the notifications floating up the screen were the usual rubbish: e-mail adverts, social media "likes" and such, but one stood out, flashing in the corner like a red alert signal: one new voicemail.

Gloria perched on the edge of the chair, biting her lip as her finger hovered above the phone screen. She glanced up at Meryl, who simply nodded, her mouth set in a grim line. Gloria pressed the symbol on the screen to play the message, desperately hoping to be comforted by the voice of Katie or Iris, but knowing in her gut it wouldn't be either of them. Her nails dug into the fabric of the chair as she listened to the cold voice seeping through the speaker, dripping with quiet rage.

'Hello Gloria.'

She felt a wave of nausea pulse through her at the sound of Greg's voice.

'I suppose you think this is over, don't you? I don't know what you think you're doing, but I've worked too hard for too long to let you ruin this for me.'

She had been right – it wasn't over.

'You haven't beaten me yet, not by a long shot. This is only the beginning. You may have forgotten that someone else shares your DNA. Someone who I'm sure will be a lot easier to...persuade.'

Gloria nearly dropped the phone as she realised who Greg was talking about.

Iris.

'Twenty-four hours. That's it. You have until nine o'clock tomorrow night to come home to me. If I don't see you by then, I'm on the next flight to Schiphol. I have connections, Gloria, and I'm capable of much more than you realise. You might have evaded me today, but there will be no mistakes next time, I promise you that.'

There was no mistaking the malice in Greg's voice. These were not empty threats.

'Oh, and one more thing. Don't bother trying to get there before me. I have friends at every single airport and, funnily enough, they're all familiar with your face. Nine o'clock tomorrow. See you soon, darling.'

The phone beeped and the message cut off, leaving Gloria in stunned silence.

She felt sick. After everything that had happened yesterday, after she'd escaped Greg's clutches, after she'd travelled across London and finally found safety, she was trapped all over again. Her new life was over before it had even begun.

She slowly lowered her phone to her lap, hands trembling so much it almost slipped out of her grasp. Meryl's voice barely penetrated her daze, seeming to come from somewhere far in the distance.

'What is it? Was it him?'

Gloria lifted her head slowly to look at Meryl, whose face was already fraught with concern. Her words came out in a choked whisper, barely audible.

'I have to go home.'

CHAPTER TWENTY-TWO

'Gloria, please, be rational!' Meryl pleaded as Gloria frantically stuffed her few scattered belongings back into her handbag. 'You can't possibly go back to him after all this.'

'I don't have a choice.' Gloria looked at Meryl through a veil of fresh tears. 'I can't risk him harming Iris.'

She closed her handbag, slumped onto the sofa and dropped her head into her hands, raking her nails through her curls. She felt utterly defeated. In less than twelve hours, she'd be right back where she started, although this time Greg would keep her on a much tighter leash. She tried to block it out, but her mind kept bringing up the image of being locked up in that spare bedroom, no longer allowed free rein of the house, and she swallowed hard to quell the bile rising in the back of her throat.

'Iris doesn't have to be a sitting duck,' Meryl continued, her voice barely breaking through Gloria's cloud of despair. 'You're not alone in this, Gloria. Can she go somewhere until you can get over there? He can't post guards at *all* the airports, surely? Gloria?'

That's it.

Gloria raised her head and wiped the tears from her eyes with the back of her hand. Of course, Greg would assume she'd try to fly out to get to Iris – he had always been wealthy, with all the privilege that came with that. It was the only way he would think of getting to Amsterdam. Gloria had other experiences entirely, and knew there was another way.

'We don't need an airport,' she said quietly, looking over at Meryl as a new wave of determination pulsed through her. 'We can go by sea.'

Meryl raised her eyebrows, clearly requiring further explanation.

'The ferry!' Gloria stood up, nervous excitement rising through her body. 'I can get the ferry from Hull to Rotterdam. And drive to Amsterdam from there.'

Meryl frowned, and Gloria's new-found optimism threatened to dim. 'Isn't that quite a lengthy journey, though? What if he reaches Iris beforehand?'

That was true. The ferry was an overnight trip, and then it was another hour at least to get from Rotterdam to the capital. Greg could be at Elias's door while she was still only halfway across the North Sea.

Elias.

Gloria picked up her phone from where she'd abandoned it on the sofa and waved it enthusiastically.

'I'll call Elias. He can move Iris somewhere safe. He has an aunt in Amsterdam, that's why he was there in the first place. I'll ask him to take her there. Right now!'

The wait for Elias to answer was agonising. Gloria paced the room with manic purpose, wanting to waste no time whatsoever now that a plan was starting to form in her mind. Greg couldn't take back control that easily; she would do everything she could to keep herself and her daughter out of his reach.

Finally, after four nerve-wracking attempts, Elias picked

up the phone.

'Gloria? What's up? You know I'm at work, right? I can't stay on long.' Elias's voice was laced with irritation.

'I won't take long. What I'm about to say is one hundred percent serious, Elias. You have to listen and do exactly what I say.'

'Okay...' The annoyance dropped from his voice as he waited for Gloria's instructions.

'Iris is in danger. You need to get her out of school and somewhere safe. To your aunt's if you can. Don't waste any time. Do it today.'

'Wait, what's happened? Are you hurt?' Elias's voice shifted to one of distress, and Gloria's heart ached a little at hearing his concern for her. 'Gloria, tell me what's going on!'

'There's no time to go into all the details. Greg is coming for her, and he's dangerous, Elias. I left him, and he tried to stop me.' She tried to keep her voice steady; this was no time to break down. She needed Elias to take this seriously. 'Now he wants Iris and you have to get her out of there, Elias, you have to!'

Gloria held her breath through several long moments as Elias considered what she had told him. Her legs turned to jelly with relief when he finally responded.

'Okay. I'll find a way to get out of work, and I'll take her to Aunt Alma's. She's away, I think, but I have her spare key. What will you do?'

'I'm coming to Amsterdam.' Her voice was firm. She would not let Greg take her daughter away from her. Not again. 'I'll be there tomorrow.'

'Gloria?' Elias's tone was one of genuine worry. 'Stay safe, please. Iris needs you.'

'You too.'

Gloria hung up the phone and looked at Meryl, whose face was set with pure determination. 'We'll save her, Gloria. I'll make sure of it.'

Gloria nodded, infinitely grateful for Meryl's continued support. She opened her mouth to speak but was cut off by the buzz of Meryl's intercom ringing out through the apartment. Meryl dashed over to the phone by the front door and quickly answered.

'Samuel? There's been a change of plan. Stay in the van. We're coming to you.'

Meryl wasted no time in preparing for the long drive to Yorkshire. In less than ten minutes, she had prepared a bag of supplies and was calling through the bedroom door for Gloria to hurry as she got dressed in some of Meryl's clothes from her youth; apparently, the woman never threw any clothing away. She had given Gloria some beautiful, flowing dresses from the sixties, along with some gorgeous loose shirts which hid the fact they were designed for a woman of a very different stature. Meryl had been somewhat of a hippy in a previous life, it seemed.

When Gloria emerged from the bedroom, she barely had time to grab her jacket and handbag before being ushered downstairs to the car park, where Samuel was waiting in the gallery van. Meryl flung her bag in the back next to the supplies Samuel had already picked up for Gloria (as instructed the previous evening) and climbed into the cab. Gloria followed suit, squeezing in besides Meryl and closing the door behind her. It wasn't going to be a comfortable journey up north, but that didn't matter.

'So,' Samuel asked, turning towards the two women,

'where to?'

'Samuel,' Meryl met his gaze, her voice stern. 'I want you to understand that you have no obligation to come with us. This is well beyond the remit of your role as my assistant, and there will be no consequences for you if you want to go home while we continue onwards. We're going to Hull, and then on to Amsterdam. Gloria's daughter is in danger, and we have to go and make sure she's all right.'

Samuel's eyes widened slightly. For a moment, a flicker of fear passed across his features before he gave a small nod. 'I'm coming with you. Let's go.'

◆ —— • ● ◆ ● • —— ◆

The drive to Hull was even more uncomfortable than Gloria had expected. Sandwiched between Meryl and the door, her back was aching before they had left the M25, and she was on the verge of faking needing the toilet just to stretch her legs when Samuel finally pulled into the motorway services somewhere along the M1. At least she, unlike Meryl, wasn't afflicted with travel sickness – one advantage of her haphazard traveller lifestyle all those years ago.

'Sorry, I didn't expect such a long drive today,' Samuel said, not taking his eyes off the road. 'I'll have to get some petrol. We can get straight back on the road if you don't want to stop and—'

'No, that's fine,' Gloria interrupted, seizing her chance. 'I think we could all do with some breakfast.'

Samuel flashed Gloria a small, knowing smile and pulled

into a parking space. She hopped out of the van barely a second after it had rolled to a stop, her back and knees singing with relief as she raised her arms above her head and stretched.

'Now,' she smiled at her two companions, 'who wants a McDonald's?'

♦———— • ● ♦ ● • ————♦

The stopover at the services was brief, but Gloria felt rejuvenated by the space and fresh air. While Samuel collected the food, she and Meryl used the free Wi-Fi to book their ferry crossing to Rotterdam. Thankfully, there were still a couple of cabins left, and Meryl had no qualms about sharing with Gloria so Samuel could have his own space – she thought forcing him to spend the night with his boss might be a little too much to ask. They had to pay more for the last minute booking, but Gloria didn't care. She'd spend every penny she had to keep Greg away from her daughter.

'Here we are!' Samuel announced, dropping a tray of hot coffee and sausage McMuffins between Meryl and Gloria. 'This should fuel us for a while, and I grabbed a few snacks and drinks from the shop for when we're back on the road.'

'You are a God-send, Samuel,' Meryl answered, not taking her eyes off her phone. 'Right, the ferry is booked. Check-in closes in around six hours, so we should have plenty of time to get to Hull.'

They ate their breakfasts in relative silence, Meryl catching up on her emails on her phone while Samuel gazed around at the other customers, people-watching. Gloria tried to concentrate on her food but felt a new wave of butterflies rise in her stomach as she considered the next stage of their journey. It had been a long time since she'd been home.

CHAPTER TWENTY-THREE

The gentle rolling rhythm of the van as it glided up the motorway had Gloria drifting into a doze. They had descended into a nervous silence as soon as they got back on the road, each of them eager to reach their destination, but powerless to get them there any quicker than the busy roads would allow.

Gloria was on the verge of unconsciousness when the loud chime of her phone ringing jolted her awake. She scrambled around to find her handbag, which had fallen on the floor of the cab, behind her feet. Pulling out her phone, a fresh wave of worry blossomed in her chest. It was Elias.

'Hello? Glor? Listen, there's a problem.'

Gloria's stomach turned to lead. *Are we already too late?*

'What's happened? Tell me Iris isn't hurt!'

'Calm down, calm down! She's fine, I think.'

'You think?' Gloria's voice rose, and Meryl and Samuel looked at her with concern in their eyes.

'The school's locked down,' Elias said, simply.

For a moment, Gloria didn't respond, dumbstruck with confusion. 'What? What do you mean?'

Elias sighed, the stress clear in his voice. 'Someone called in and said there was a shooter. They've locked the whole campus down until security and the police do a full sweep and can be sure it's safe.'

'A shooter?'

Gloria's mind began to race, conjuring up worst-case scenarios of fallen teenagers and teachers, riddled with bullets and bathed in blood. Iris alone and terrified or, much worse, hurt, or even dead. She gulped for air as her chest began to constrict, squeezing the air out of her lungs.

'Where are they? Did they get into the school? Has anyone been hurt?'

'Glor, Glor, calm down. The head of the school is in regular contact with us, and they're pretty sure it's a hoax. It was an anonymous call from an unknown number, and no one's been hurt as far as they know. But they have to take these precautions just in case. It's a really safe school, Glor, that's one of the reasons we chose it.'

Gloria barely heard the last few words. Her mind was fixated one on the one phrase which had stood out to her.

Anonymous call from an unknown number.

'Greg.' Gloria whispered, barely audible, as she stared forward in disbelief, her blood running cold. 'Elias, I don't like this. He's trying to keep her there, I know it.'

'Do you really think he's capable of that?' Elias didn't sound at all convinced. 'It seems a bit extreme, Glor. He's just one man, after all.'

Gloria knew it sounded farfetched, but it was the only explanation, and she knew deep down in her gut that it was true. Things like this didn't happen at Iris's school. And, after all, Greg had said he had connections – what if they reached all the way to Amsterdam?

'It might sound crazy, but you didn't hear what he said, the threats he made.' She took a deep breath in a feeble attempt to steady her fraying nerves. 'Stay on standby, and as soon as they ease the lockdown, get her out of there and to Alma's. Please, do whatever it takes.'

Elias was silent for a moment, but when his voice returned, it brimmed with determination. 'Right. Don't worry, Gloria, I won't leave here without her. I'm as scared as you are.'

'Of course, I know. Please, message me as soon as she's with you.' Gloria hesitated for a moment. 'Look after yourself too, Elias.'

A soft chuckle at the other end of the phone brought a familiar heat to Gloria's cheeks that she hadn't experienced for a long time. 'You too, Glor. Stay safe.'

Gloria clenched her eyes shut, flinching as Meryl slipped a caring arm around her shoulders. She sagged against her friend as she pulled her close and squeezed her shoulder.

'She'll be okay, dear. Her dad is there, and we'll be there soon.'

Gloria's resolve finally broke, and she sobbed silently into Meryl's shoulder, no longer able to hold back the flood of emotion she'd been struggling to contain since this ordeal began. It just wasn't fair, any of it. This wasn't what she had planned! She should have still been at home, making her final preparations to fly out and meet Katie in Paris.

Katie.

In all the chaos, Gloria had completely forgotten to let Katie know about the change of plans. She was in Paris now, getting ready for Gloria to arrive, blissfully ignorant of the current situation. She was in no fit state to call her now, but she had to say something. Katie had been the whole reason she had Meryl here to support her now. Gloria owed her everything. She unlocked her phone and typed out a message, squinting to see through the resurfacing tears.

Greg knows. He's after Iris and I have to go to Amsterdam NOW. I'll explain everything later when she's safe. Thank you so much for everything. I hope I can repay you someday.

She'd see her friend again, she was sure of it.

The afternoon crawled forwards with agonising sluggishness, yet Gloria fidgeted nervously as Hull began to appear on the motorway signs. She hadn't been back to her hometown since the night she'd escaped almost twenty-five years ago and crossed the North Sea to freedom. She had vowed to never return, and at the time had seen no reason why she ever would. Hitchhiking through Europe as a teenager had been difficult, and terrifying at times, but had all been worth it to get away from the hell she'd left behind. She found her thoughts drifting to her mother, wondering where she was now, whether she was even still alive.

No. I'm not going there.

She closed her eyes and took a few slow breaths in an attempt to empty her mind and steady her quickening heartbeat. Soon enough, they'd be through the city and out the other side, back on the open sea. She formed a picture of it in her mind: the rolling sapphire waves breaking over the bow of the ship, the tang of salt tingling in her nostrils, the wide expanse of the sea stretching all around, promising a second chance.

God, she missed it.

A sharp jolt dragged Gloria out of her daydream as the van rapidly decelerated and she lurched forward in her seat. The seatbelt slammed into her chest and knocked the wind out of her. Samuel stamped his foot a few times, eyes widening as the vehicle failed to respond. He gripped the steering wheel with both hands as he struggled to manoeuvre across the lanes towards the safety of the hard shoulder, cars thundering past on either side of the van.

'What's happening?' Gloria shouted, holding on to the door as the van swung to the left, narrowly avoiding a lorry.

'I'm not sure!' Samuel yelled over the horns of the surrounding vehicles, protesting against his erratic driving. 'I think the breaks have gone, and—WOAH!'

Samuel jerked the steering wheel to get out of the way of a fast-approaching SUV, and the world was thrown into slow motion. The van went into a spin, the surrounding carriageway a blur of moving colours through the windows. Gloria closed her eyes as they careered into the hard shoulder. They span onwards until the van finally reached the crash barrier, the bonnet crumpling with a sickening crunch. Gloria, Meryl and Samuel were thrown forwards into their seatbelts, the air knocked out of their lungs on impact.

Gloria rubbed her temples in a futile attempt to stop the ringing in her head. The van may have slowed initially, but they'd been hurtling down the fast lane when disaster struck, so they'd still crashed with considerable force. A dull ache throbbed in Gloria's chest where the seatbelt had hit her body like a hammer. As her head began to clear, she became vaguely aware of Meryl's struggling voice to the right of her.

'I...can't breathe...'

Gloria opened her eyes, and a wave of nausea pulsed through her as her sight adjusted to the van's new position. Through the windscreen, she saw a steep bank descending into a sprawling area of woodland. Her chest tightened as she considered how dire their situation could have been, had they not stopped where they had. She released her seatbelt, easing the pressure on her lungs, and turned to see Meryl clutching her chest.

'Meryl? Are you okay? Samuel, unfasten her belt!'

Samuel sat fixed in place, staring forwards, knuckles paling under his iron grip on the steering wheel. *He's in shock.* Gloria was going to have to sort this out by herself. She reached across Meryl's body, taking care not to put any weight on her, and slowly released her seatbelt. Meryl seemed to melt into her seat, rubbing her chest and gasping for air. Gloria gently took her hand.

'It's all right, Meryl. Take some deep breaths. I'll let some fresh air in.'

She tried to open the passenger door, but it wouldn't budge. They were trapped. She had to get Samuel moving, or they were going nowhere.

'Samuel? Samuel!' It was no good. He wasn't listening.

Gloria pivoted in her seat and reached over to him, placing her free hand softly on his arm. She squeezed it gently.

'Samuel? Please, I need your help now. Meryl needs your help. Please listen to me.'

Tears were beginning to well behind Gloria's eyes when

Samuel finally blinked and turned to face her, eyes wide and glistening.

'It's okay. We're all okay.' Gloria moved her hand to his and slowly removed his fingers from the steering wheel. 'But we need to get Meryl some fresh air. Can you open your door for me, please?'

'I'm sorry...I'm so sorry, Gloria, I panicked, I—'

'It's okay, Samuel.' She squeezed his hand and fixed her gaze on his. 'But I need you to help us now. We'll worry about everything else once we get out of the van.'

How am I so calm? Gloria had become so used to being panicked and anxious lately, she was surprising herself. *Maybe I'm in shock, too.*

Samuel nodded slowly and released his other hand from the steering wheel. His fingers trembled as he fumbled with the door handle. To Gloria's great relief, the door eventually creaked open a crack, giving way and swinging open when Samuel gave it a shove with his shoulder. He stumbled out onto the hard shoulder, recoiling as a large lorry roared past a mere six feet away. The sound was deafening, and Gloria became acutely aware of how vulnerable they were. They needed to get out of this van and safely behind the barrier before they were wiped out completely.

'Samuel, help Meryl out of the van and get behind the barrier, quickly!'

Samuel nodded, their precarious situation seeming to shake him out of his stupor. Reaching into the van, he took Meryl by the hand and eased her out onto the hard shoulder. Her breathing was starting to steady, but her face was abnormally pale, and she looked ready to drop at any moment. Gloria followed behind, a gentle hand on Meryl's shoulder.

'Thank you,' Meryl breathed, flashing Gloria a small but gracious smile.

Together, the three of them slowly made their way to the crash barrier. Once they had helped each other over and onto the top of the grassy bank, the adrenaline finally drained from Gloria's body, and she slumped to the ground in a heap.

They were safe – but now what?

CHAPTER TWENTY-FOUR

'No, that's not good enough I'm afraid – we're on the side of the bloody motorway!'

Meryl paced up and down along the bank, one hand holding the phone to her ear while the other gestured wildly with frustration. Gloria sat with Samuel on the grass, safely away from the speeding traffic, like children waiting for their parents to get them back on the road to some seaside holiday. Gloria looked over to Samuel, who finally seemed to be recovering from the shock of the crash.

'How are you doing?' she asked, willing him to look at her, but his eyes remained fixed on his hands, fingers tightly laced on his lap.

'Okay, I suppose,' he muttered, barely audible over the roar of the busy carriageway.

'Samuel.' Gloria leaned forward until he finally met her gaze, his warm, dark eyes shining with the threat of tears. 'It's okay to not be okay. Talk to me, please. It'll help us both.'

Samuel hesitated. 'I just feel so...stupid.' His voice cracked a little. 'I panicked and put us all in danger. I could have killed us, killed Meryl! You saw how bad she looked. All because of me.'

He dropped his head again, and Gloria noticed a few spots of moisture drop onto his jeans as he tried to hide his tears.

She reached out and gave his arm a squeeze, leaving her hand there when he made no effort to shake her off.

'The accident was not your fault. You reacted the same way anyone would, and if anything, you probably saved our lives by reacting so quickly. You haven't seen me drive. I'd have probably ploughed us into a bus or something.'

Samuel let out a small laugh and wiped his eyes with the back of his hand. 'It's just...Meryl. She puts a lot of trust in me, especially considering I don't have much experience yet. I just...I hope I haven't lost that.'

Gloria glanced over at Meryl, still gesturing emphatically as she argued with the breakdown company.

'You really care what she thinks of you, don't you?'

Samuel shrugged, a small smile playing on his lips as Meryl insisted on speaking to the operator's supervisor. 'It's hard not to. She's an incredible boss.'

Gloria couldn't help but smile over at Meryl herself. *She's an incredible person.*

'I wouldn't worry,' she said, turning back to Samuel and placing a reassuring hand on his knee. 'Someone like her doesn't give up on people that easily. I'm sure of it.'

Minutes later, Meryl hung up and strode back over to them, looking very pleased with herself. Samuel and Gloria jumped up, keen to find out what was happening.

'Recovery are on their way!' she announced, clapping her hands together enthusiastically.

Gloria's heart leapt. Finally, some good news! She looked down at her own phone – check-in closed in three hours. 'How long did they say they'll be?'

'After a lengthy discussion, they agreed to come right away.'

Gloria let out a sigh of relief. 'Oh, thank God. We'll be in Hull in no time, then.'

Meryl frowned a little at that. 'Well...not quite.'

Gloria's stomach dropped. *What now?*

'Apparently, my cover will only get us towed to a nearby garage, and not all the way to Hull. I tried to fight it, but no dice. It's right there in the Ts and Cs, unfortunately.'

Gloria's chest tightened as anxiety began to flood her body. 'What are we going to do? We're still over an hour away from Hull!' She threw her arms up in exasperation and clasped her head in her hands.

'Don't panic!' Meryl grabbed her arms gently and slowly lowered them to her sides. 'Let's all be calm, and just think this thing through.' Meryl was silent for a few moments as she considered their options. Her eyes fell on Gloria as an idea seemed to strike her. 'Gloria, you're Northern, right?'

Gloria cringed. How many more years would it take to finally shake off the remnants of that accent? 'Originally, yes. Why?'

'Do you know anyone nearby who can help us? Tow us somewhere or give us a lift to Hull? I think we're between Sheffield and Doncaster.'

'No.'

'Are you sure? It only has to be—'

'No, Meryl, I don't!'

Meryl's eyes widened, taken aback by Gloria's sudden anger. Several long seconds of silence followed, punctuated only by the sound of the rumbling traffic as cars and lorries sped by. Samuel scuffed his feet on the ground, his eyes avoiding either of the two women. Gloria looked down at her hands, unable to maintain eye contact any longer.

'Okay,' Meryl finally said, lifting her chin and walking back to the van, where she proceeded to climb in and rummage through the glove box. Gloria sighed and rubbed her eyes, a steady stream of guilt rising up inside her.

That wasn't fair. She doesn't know.

She followed Meryl to the van and quietly climbed in beside her, putting a tentative hand on her friend's shoulder. The older woman turned around slowly, eyebrows raised.

'Sorry, Meryl. I didn't mean to snap at you, especially after you've been so good to me. It's just...' Gloria's eyes began to burn, threatening tears, but she held them back. 'Well, I cut all ties with home when I left. There are no friends around here for me anymore.'

Meryl nodded, and Gloria was relieved to see her expression soften, her warm, kind eyes returning. 'You have friends here, dear. We only want what's best. Try to remember that. Apology accepted.'

Gloria sat in silence, too embarrassed to say any more. She watched as Meryl drew an old battered road map out from under the pile of papers and envelopes and flipped through the pages, a look of purpose fixed in her eyes.

'Aha!' She grinned, planting a finger in the middle of a page.

'What is it?' Gloria asked, leaning over to look. All she could see was Sheffield city centre. 'I don't understand.'

Meryl looked up at Gloria, a mischievous smile on her face. 'I think our recovery driver will find the closest local garage happens to be right by Sheffield Train Station. We'll be back on the road – well, tracks – in no time!'

◆———— • ● ◆ ● • ————◆

'Wait, wait, wait!' Gloria shouted as she sprinted down the platform, Meryl's bag threatening to fall off her shoulder with every pound of her foot on the hard concrete.

Meryl had been true to her word, weaving her magic on the hapless young recovery driver once the van was finally loaded onto his truck until he was offering to drop them off right at the station entrance. Gloria had watched in awe, mystified that anyone could possess such charisma when she herself was such a failure with words.

She reached the train with only a couple of minutes left until departure, straddling the doorway with one foot still on the platform as she watched Samuel drag Meryl towards the carriage. She wasn't frail by any means, but Gloria guessed it had been many years since she had needed to sprint to avoid missing a connection – and she certainly wasn't dressed for running in her smart black heels. Gloria glanced up at the digital display board, the seconds slipping away as the time of departure drew closer.

She resisted the urge to scream for them to hurry as they jogged to the train, faces flushed with exertion. As they drew closer, her fingers twitched with the desire to drag them into the carriage, but she fought against it, clenching her fists.

They're going as fast as they can.

Finally, they stepped through the door and onto the train, with less than a minute to spare. The three of them walked through the busy carriage in search of vacant seats. Rush hour was just beginning, and the train was packed, mostly with tired-looking commuters and students, wanting nothing more than a quiet journey home where they could finally relax. Luckily, there was one free table at the very back of the train, littered with old coffee cups and newspapers.

'I am not built for running,' Meryl sighed as she threw herself into a seat, wiping her brow with a handkerchief. 'And would you look at the state of this table? Samuel, dear, would you mind throwing away this mess?'

Gloria didn't care about the state of the table. As Samuel began clearing the debris away, she sank down into her seat, a wave of relief washing over here. The day might not be going as originally planned, but they were finally on the move again. She rested her head against the window, and as the train lurched into motion, she allowed a small smile to cross her lips.

I'm coming, Iris.

CHAPTER TWENTY-FIVE

Gloria had a sudden urge to close her eyes as the taxi trundled away from the Hull Paragon Interchange and headed out into the bustling city centre, but she forced herself to look out of the window – to face the past.

Hull had certainly changed in the last twenty years, now awash with new shops, heaving pubs and busy restaurants, but that did not still the butterflies stirring in Gloria's stomach, building in intensity with each recognised landmark. On the streets, the locals went about their daily business, walking home from work or heading out for dinner, enjoying their day-to-day lives without a care in the world. Gloria envied them; her time here had been an altogether different experience.

Her resolve finally faltered as the car left the centre of the city and headed eastwards in the direction of the docks. The imposing silhouette of HMP Hull came into focus, stark and cold against the otherwise perfect summer sky, and her eyes clenched shut before she could stop herself. She had hoped to never see the prison again, to cleanse all memory of the place from her mind forever. Seeing it now sent a familiar chill down her spine that she had almost managed to forget.

He's dead, remember? Dead.

As much as Gloria tried not to think about her mother, she had repressed the memory of her father altogether, preferring not to acknowledge he'd even existed. Faced with the scene of their last meeting, however, Gloria found the memory creeping back. It hadn't been enough for her mother to continually welcome him back to their grotty little flat, no matter what he did to them; she'd then insisted on taking Gloria with her to visit him in prison. She couldn't have been more than ten years old, and the place had terrified her. As her mother dragged her through the bleak, echoing corridors, she had screamed – no, she had *begged* – to go home. She didn't want to see him, he scared her, but her cries fell on deaf ears. Her mother had been the one to pay for her mistake, however, and Gloria had to be whisked away by security as a group of officers pried that man's fingers from around her mother's throat.

Forgiveness was impossible, but she could forget if she just tried hard enough.

Gloria's heart soared when she finally felt the taxi turn off the dual carriageway, and her eyes fluttered open to behold the great blue and white ferry looming before them. Some might have considered it an eyesore, but to Gloria it was the picture of freedom.

She felt a familiar tingle spread over her skin as she stepped out of the taxi into the brisk air of King George Dock. Despite the dazzling summer sunshine, Gloria was taken back to the last time she stood in this spot, the hood of her threadbare winter coat pulled down to protect her face from the biting October wind.

The car park had been eerily quiet, empty aside from a handful of cars scattered across the cracked, grey concrete. Gloria's feet ached from the long walk to the dock; the handful of notes she had managed to smuggle out of the flat covered her crossing, but she couldn't spare any of it for a taxi, or even a bus ride.

It had been now or never when she had been left alone in the flat for the first time in days. Her mother had looked almost cheerful when she told Gloria she would soon be joining her, whether she liked it or not, and Gloria could not let that happen. She wouldn't end up like *her*. It was a stroke of pure luck that her mother had needed to leave the flat before putting Gloria to work. A golden opportunity she would grab with both hands.

Gloria took a deep breath and shook her head, shedding the cobwebs of the past. Soon, they would be on the water and out of this wretched place. It would be no loss to Gloria if she never saw the city again.

After negotiating her way through check-in and security, it was as if a veil of dread fell away from her as she stepped from the terminal and left Hull behind, hopefully forever.

The ferry was almost exactly how she remembered it. It was a vast ship, with corridors snaking off from the large, colourful foyer area, still sporting the same hideously patterned carpet she remembered from her previous trip all those years ago. With check-in about to close, it was bustling with life, full of eager families and party groups kicking off their holidays early with some onboard festivities. Gloria could hear excited chatter echoing down every passageway. She ached to feel something close to that.

'Let's find our cabins, shall we?' Meryl asked cheerfully, seemingly as happy as Gloria to be leaving England behind. 'I think we're this way.'

Gloria and Samuel followed Meryl's lead into the nearest lift, which was unfortunately crowded with people. She tried to avoid the gaze of the holidaymakers who had packed themselves into the claustrophobic little box with them, all beaming with joy as they speculated what activities they might get up to in Amsterdam. Gloria didn't want to hear about their holiday plans, and she willed the lift to hurry as it glided up to a part of the ship she had never visited before: the Premier Deck.

Their booking being last minute, the trio had had no choice but to opt for premium cabins; they were the only ones still available. Gloria had been privately relieved. She had stayed in a standard bunk last time, the cheapest available and all she could afford with the cash she had managed to scrape together at home, and they were extremely short on space. At least she and Meryl wouldn't be on top of each other in their twin room. When they reached their corridor, Samuel bid them goodbye and headed onwards to find his own cabin, leaving Gloria and Meryl to themselves.

'Shall we?' Meryl smiled, opening their cabin door and striding inside, immediately flopping down onto the nearest bed. 'What a day!'

Gloria followed suit, sitting heavily on her own bed and kicking off her shoes, thankful for a moment of quiet respite after the chaos of the day thus far. She could hardly believe the situation she found herself in. How simple life had been just a few short weeks ago, or so she had thought. She raked her fingers through her hair and rubbed her scalp, hoping to somehow relieve her anxiety, but it didn't help. Easing back onto the bed, she sunk down into the soft duvet and allowed her eyelids to flutter shut.

Gloria had barely begun to doze when a loud chime from her phone knocked her awake, and she sat bolt upright.

Elias. She scrambled onto the floor and felt around under the bed until she found her forgotten handbag and retrieved her phone. A shock of relief ran through her as she read the message which flashed up on the screen.

> They've finally let her out. On our way to Alma's, will call you when we're there. E x

'Thank God,' Gloria breathed. Before she could stop herself, she brought the phone to her lips and kissed the screen. For a second, she felt embarrassed, but this soon vanished as a soft snore from Meryl's bed confirmed that she hadn't seen a thing.

I need to calm down.

She had been tightly wound all day and was starting to panic at every little thing.

If I carry on like this, I'll have a nervous breakdown.

She decided to take advantage of the alone time, and the free toiletries on offer in their more expensive cabin, and take a hot shower to try to relax and clear her head.

The en suite bathroom was tiny, as she'd expected, but it was clean and quiet, and that's all she needed right now. As the hot water soaked through her hair and down her body, she felt some of the tension fall from her. The pure escapism and isolation which could be found in a shower cubicle had always been close to therapy for Gloria. There was no one there to judge her, no outside worries, no distractions, nothing. As a child, it was sometimes the only place she felt clean and safe. Well, before her mother broke the bathroom lock. She could never feel safe after that; not until she had escaped.

Alone and lost in a meditative state under the flow of the water, Gloria lost all track of time. She was loathe to leave the warmth and comfort of her safe haven, but her rumbling stomach eventually forced her to relent. Some of the food Samuel had bought at the service station was with their bags in the bedroom. She would have to go back to reality to sate her hunger.

She emerged from the en suite, enveloped in a fluffy white towel, to find Meryl awake and changed into a sweeping, long-sleeved black dress, applying makeup as she studied her reflection in a hand mirror.

'Ah, Gloria, dear!' she announced without taking her eyes off the mirror. 'I thought we could all do with cheering up a little, so I've asked Samuel to meet us at the restaurant for dinner. Get yourself ready. The first round's on me.'

◆———— • ● ◆ ● • ———— ◆

Gloria had to admit, it was nice to return to some semblance of normality, even if only for a few hours. The meal had been surprisingly delicious, and Meryl had bought them a bottle of Riesling to share, which was going down very well. Gloria and Samuel had shared some light-hearted conversation about their favourite artists and paintings, and she had been delighted to hear they shared a love of David Hockney. Maybe it was the wine emboldening him, but Samuel was finally starting to come out of his shell, and Gloria was thoroughly enjoying his company.

Meryl, however, didn't seem to be having such a good time. Unlike Gloria, she had little prior experience of travelling by sea, and her complexion was becoming decidedly greener as the boat gently rocked with the rhythm of the crashing waves outside. The plate of risotto in front of her sat virtually untouched, although she had managed to polish off a large glass of wine, which didn't seem to be helping. When the waiter appeared and offered her the dessert menu, she shook her head and rose unsteadily from the table.

'I'm afraid I have to retire to my cabin – I seem to have left my sea legs at home.' She steadied herself using her chair and placed some cash on the table. 'You two continue your meal, and we'll catch up at breakfast. Goodnight!'

Gloria couldn't help but giggle as she watched Meryl meander out of the restaurant, leaving Samuel and her alone with the waiter.

'Would you like dessert?' the waiter asked cheerfully, looking equally amused by Meryl's sudden departure.

'What the hell!' Gloria took a menu from him and began reading. 'You only live once, right? I'll have the crème brûlée. Samuel?'

Samuel flashed a wide smile back at Gloria, his eyes bright. 'Make that two.' He lowered his voice as the waiter retreated from the table. 'I've never had one before, so it's on you if I hate it.'

Gloria laughed and gave Samuel a little shove on the shoulder. It was so refreshing to be able to joke around at dinner. She felt surprisingly comfortable with Samuel, considering she had known him such a short time. He was warm and kind, and she could be herself around him. Dinners with Greg had always felt like a test she was barely scraping through without failing.

As the desserts arrived, Samuel ordered another round of drinks and studied the dish before him. He pushed at it tentatively with his spoon. 'So...is it supposed to be hard?'

Gloria laughed so loudly the diners at the nearest table turned to stare at the commotion. She took no notice – she was having fun.

'It's just caramelised sugar on top.' She cracked the top of hers with her spoon and took a mouthful of the newly exposed creamy dessert. 'See?'

Samuel smacked his forehead in embarrassment and shook his head. 'Oh, dear,' he laughed. 'You can't take me anywhere.'

They finished their dessert in a silence which felt surprisingly comfortable, considering they barely knew each other. When the drinks arrived, Samuel held up his wine glass, and Gloria happily obliged, clinking it against her own.

'I'm not usually much of a drinker,' Samuel confessed, taking a small sip of the amber liquid. 'But after the last twenty-four hours, I think we both need a few stiff drinks!'

Gloria smiled and nodded, not wanting to admit that she would regularly have multiple glasses of wine in the evening. She had tried to cut down several times, to no avail. She seemed to recall Greg revelling in each of her failures, affirming his position as the superior half of the couple.

'Well, this is delicious,' she finally said, taking a sip. 'Meryl has excellent taste in wine.'

'She has excellent taste in everything, it seems.' Samuel smiled at Gloria, blushing as he averted his eyes to peer awkwardly into his glass.

Gloria opened her mouth to ask what Samuel had meant by that, but was cut short by the sudden sound of her phone ringing in her handbag.

'Oh, sorry. Let me check that.' She fished her phone out of her bag, preparing to hang up on whoever was interrupting their dinner.

That was until she saw Greg's name flashing on the screen, and her stomach turned to ice.

Greg's deadline.

She had enjoyed dinner so much she'd lost track of time and completely forgotten Greg had been waiting for her to be home by nine. He must be livid.

'Sorry, I should take this.' She stood up and dashed out of the restaurant before Samuel could respond, hurrying to the end of the corridor where no one would be around to overhear. Her gut clenched so tightly she thought she might vomit as she answered, trying to keep her voice steady.

'Hello, Greg.'

'You've disappointed me, Gloria.' His voice was hard and edged with malice. 'You should have been home by now.'

Gloria opened her mouth to respond, but the words wouldn't come. It was as if her throat had closed up on hearing Greg's voice. She waited in silence for him to continue, hoping to God his ears didn't pick up on her quickening breath.

'Not talking to your husband, sweetheart?' Gloria sensed a smirk in his tone. 'That's fine. You don't need to say anything, just listen. I gave you a chance to see sense and come home, and you've thrown that back in my face. Well, I warned you.'

'What will you do?' Gloria managed to squeak out, already dreading his response.

'Oh, so you *are* there? Good. I didn't want it to come to

this, Gloria. I gave you the chance to come back and put this ugliness behind us, but it looks like you want to do this the hard way. I've been kind so far but, as soon as I hang up, I'm cutting you off – and I don't mean just the bank accounts. That phone in your hand? That's mine, registered under *my* name. One word from me, and it's blocked, disconnected, gone. So, good luck darling. And don't worry, I'll be sure to say hello to Iris for you.'

With that, he was gone, leaving Gloria alone in the corridor, speechless and...disconnected.

CHAPTER TWENTY-SIX

Gloria threw back the last mouthful of wine, barely tasting the liquid as it hit the back of her throat. She didn't even know what kind of wine it was. When she'd sought sanctuary in a dark corner of the Irish bar, she'd simply asked the barman for whatever was cheapest. She didn't care what it tasted like as long as it numbed her from the pain of reality for a while.

Greg had been true to his word – she was already locked out of her phone, and with that, he had severed her ties to the rest of the world. She didn't know if Elias and Iris had made it to Alma's, she didn't know if Iris knew she was on her way, she didn't even know if Iris was okay. Was she panicking? How much had Elias told her? Gloria hoped she was doing as she was told. Iris could be extremely stubborn.

As the warmth of the alcohol spread through her body, she tried to force herself to be optimistic. Iris would be okay. She was a smart girl. *At least, I think she's smart.* She certainly attended the best school possible. In truth, Gloria hadn't asked Iris about her grades for a while. In fact, she couldn't remember the last time they'd spoken about school. She had spent all these years worrying about giving her daughter the best possible start in life and then hadn't even bothered to get to know her.

'God, I'm a terrible mum,' she groaned, burying her head in her hands.

'No one who travels across the country, and then across the North Sea, just to make sure their daughter is safe, is a terrible mum.'

Gloria lifted her head, tears pricking the backs of her eyes, and saw Samuel standing at the other side of the table, brown eyes tinged with sympathy. 'Is this seat taken?'

Gloria smiled, wiping her eyes with the back of her hand, which she regretted when she returned it to her wine glass and saw the resulting black smudges of mascara. *I'm such a mess.*

'No, feel free.' She gestured at the seat opposite her, hoping the dim lighting hid the worst of her smeared makeup. 'How did you know I was here?'

'Just a lucky guess, I suppose.' He glanced away as he sat, deliberately avoiding eye contact. *He knew I'd be drinking*, Gloria thought with a pang of embarrassment. He barely knew her and had already clocked her as having a problem. 'Do you want to talk about it?'

'I'm not sure it'll help,' she muttered, swirling the last remaining dregs in her wine glass. It turned out the barman had chosen a white wine. 'Everything's such a mess.'

Samuel didn't respond. Instead, he surveyed the room, eyes scanning the few happy couples and groups of friends scattered throughout the bar, totally carefree and excited about their upcoming holidays. Gloria wished she could share their enthusiasm. When she had last made this journey, she had been frightened, but also full of optimism and excitement to be finally leaving her hellish life behind. This time, she didn't even have that.

'Come on.' Samuel broke the silence between them, standing and reaching out a hand.

'What?' Gloria frowned up at him in confusion, but all he offered was a mischievous smile.

She slowly raised her hand and, as their skin touched, she felt a wave of goosebumps spread up the back of her arms. Samuel's fingers closed around hers, and he pulled her up out of her chair and towards the exit. Within minutes, they were in the lift, flying upwards towards the top of the ship.

'Where are we going?' Gloria asked, her head spinning a little from the alcohol coursing through her body combined with the sudden vertical movement.

'I have an idea that might cheer you up.'

I seriously doubt it, Gloria thought, but Samuel looked so sincere, she smiled back at him with all the eagerness she could muster. Unfortunately, it wasn't very much, but Samuel didn't seem deterred.

When the lift finally came to a stop, they stepped out into the hallway to face a large set of sleek glass double-doors. They were emblazoned with the words "Sky Lounge".

'Another bar?' Gloria asked slowly, her stomach dropping. 'Look, I know I drink a lot, but—'

'Just wait.' Samuel laughed, shaking his head at her.

He held one of the glass doors open and gestured for her to go through. She complied, appreciating the change of scenery to a much more elegant atmosphere, but concerned Samuel thought she was nothing more than a sad alcoholic. She was surprised, however, when he led her past the bar to another set of glass doors at the far end of the room. As the door swung inwards, the breath was knocked from her lungs as she was hit with a gust of brisk, cold wind. Samuel grinned as he took her hand again and led her outside.

They stood on the top deck of the ship, looking out over the railings at the vast expanse of the North Sea, the crashing waves roaring towards them from beyond the horizon. There was no land to be seen, just the roiling indigo water, its surface laced with the dancing reflection of the soft moonlight. Gloria closed her eyes and took a deep breath in. She could taste the salt in the fresh, cool air, and it was delicious. The wind tugged her hair behind her, and for a moment, she felt like she could rise off the deck and fly away.

If only.

The cold of the night air should have bothered her, but as the goose pimples blossomed over her bare skin, Gloria felt alive, more alive than she had felt in a long time. The sea breeze, the rise and fall of the passing waves, the chill of the clear, crisp summer night – it was perfect. She could have stayed in this moment forever. She reluctantly opened her eyes and turned to Samuel, who was quietly watching her with a look of intense interest.

'How did you know?' she asked quietly, the crash of the waves almost drowning out her words.

Samuel gave a small smile. 'Your paintings,' he said simply. 'They spoke of the sea, like you had this unresolved, aching passion for it. That's how I interpreted it, anyway. I'm quite often wrong about these things.'

Gloria smiled and looped her arm through his, drawing him closer. 'No, you were absolutely right. Thank you so much.'

They stood in silence for a few minutes, revelling in the

peace of being alone and spared the worries the rest of the world brought with it.

'I've been here before, you know,' Gloria said quietly, leaning forward onto the railing. The cold metal bit at her bare flesh, but she didn't mind. 'On this ship, I mean.'

'Really? When?'

Gloria sensed Samuel turning to face her, but she kept staring forwards, into the waves. Somehow, it made it easier.

'When I was sixteen. Not much older than Iris, I suppose.'

'Family holiday?'

Gloria couldn't help but laugh. Samuel was so naive. It was endearing, really, and Gloria wished she'd had a chance to hang on to such innocence. 'No...not exactly. I was leaving home, permanently. My mum...' She hesitated but compelled herself to continue. She had to talk about it sooner or later. 'My mum was a drug addict and...well, it made life at home impossible. Especially...especially when she started dealing.'

Gloria felt hot tears bubble up behind her eyelids but didn't try to hold them back. Even revealing that small fact felt like a huge weight had been lifted from her, a weight she was so accustomed to bearing, she had forgotten it even existed.

'I'm so sorry, Gloria, I had no idea.'

'It's okay.'

'No, it's not okay.' Samuel placed a hand on Gloria's arm and turned her to face him, his face serious. 'You've been through some really hard stuff, and you're allowed to feel angry about it.'

Gloria met Samuel's gaze. She had spent her life keeping her problems to herself, locking away her painful past in a corner of her mind she never let herself re-explore. It had seemed like the right thing to do, but looking into Samuel's warm, dark eyes, she found herself wanting to finally let it go. The question was whether she was brave enough to finally do it.

'Thank you. You're right. It's just...difficult. I've held it in for so long.' The floodgates opened, and fresh tears erupted down Gloria's face. She was sure that, by now, she must look an absolute mess, but she didn't care.

'I understand.' Samuel brushed a tear from Gloria's cheek with his thumb. His skin was soft, his touch remarkably tender. 'But when you feel ready, if you need someone to talk to, I want you to know I'm here.'

Gloria didn't know what to say. This young man, who she had known for only a few days, was showing her more compassion than her husband had given her throughout their entire marriage. She now realised how truly lonely she had been these past few years. Despite the chill of the wind caressing her hair, Gloria's skin flushed with a heat that had nothing to do with the alcohol coursing through her veins.

The pair stood in silence, eyes locked on each other, and Gloria became increasingly aware of how close Samuel was, his dark, full lips now only inches away from her own. Her heart hammered against her ribs, and her lips parted to release her quickening breath. Samuel's fingers tightened slightly around Gloria's arms, and she let herself be pulled even closer. Her eyes had just begun to flutter shut when a new voice spoke out behind them.

'Sorry, guys, we're closing up now. You'll have to go back downstairs.'

Just like that, the tension vanished. Gloria and Samuel stepped back from one another, and Gloria began wiping the tears from her face in an effort to hide her glowing cheeks. The barman held open the door for them, and Gloria thought she caught him offering Samuel a wink as he passed through. She suddenly felt very foolish.

They travelled down to the Premier Deck in silence, and it was to Gloria's great relief when they finally approached the cabin she shared with Meryl.

'Well...I guess this is goodnight,' Samuel said, offering an awkward smile as his gaze finally met Gloria's again.

Words failed her, but thankfully a small smile in return seemed to be enough, and Samuel continued onwards towards his own cabin. When he eventually rounded the corner and passed out of sight, Gloria closed her eyes and leaned her head back against the door.

She felt so *stupid*.

CHAPTER TWENTY-SEVEN

For the first time in her life, Gloria was grateful for a hangover.

The ferry was sailing a lot more smoothly come morning, which meant Meryl was back to her old self and eager for breakfast.

'I've texted Samuel to meet me at the buffet at seven. Would you like to join us?'

Gloria's insides churned at the thought of seeing Samuel again after she had embarrassed herself the night before. She wriggled further under the covers and affected a pathetic whimper. 'I think I'll have to give breakfast a miss,' she groaned. 'I've got a terrible headache.'

Meryl turned from the mirror, where she was already fully dressed and applying her lipstick. 'Oh, dear! Well, there are painkillers in my bag if you need them. Drink plenty of water. I'll be back by eight when we need to be ready to go.'

Gloria let out a sigh of relief as Meryl rose to leave with no further questions. She hoped Samuel would be discreet. After all, nothing had really happened.

Then why do I feel so ridiculous?

She shook her head and sat up in bed. She didn't have time to feel sorry for herself – she had to get to Iris and make sure she was okay.

By the time Meryl returned from breakfast, Gloria had managed to pull on some clothes and make herself look somewhat presentable. She helped Meryl pack up the remainder of her things, and they left the cabin together to see Samuel heading up the corridor towards them.

Oh, shit.

She tried to hurry Meryl onwards, but it was too late. She had already spotted her assistant and was enthusiastically waving him over.

'Samuel! Excellent, we can head to the bus together. Let's go.'

Gloria offered Samuel a quick, polite wave and scurried to the head of the group, avoiding eye contact. Meryl didn't seem to notice and continued walking between the awkward pair, regaling them with the story of when the Hofmann-Mills Gallery was first erected in Amsterdam. Gloria wished she had the wherewithal to listen to what would ordinarily be a subject of great interest to her, but through the mist of her hangover, she could think of only one thing: Iris.

The bus from Rotterdam was comfortable enough, but as one might have expected, it was packed to the brim with excited revellers, none of whom seemed to be suffering from their exploits of the previous night. Gloria secured herself a seat between Meryl and the window and settled in for the long ride to the capital.

Despite the pounding in her head, she was full of nervous energy, unable to keep her hands still.

It's fine. It's going to be fine.

Then why was she so anxious? She would be reunited with Iris and Elias soon, and they could figure everything out then. All that mattered was being with them again. She was so close now, but if anything, that only heightened her worry. Cold dread pooled in her stomach; something just didn't feel right. She had begun picking at her nails when a small hand reached across and gently held her hands still.

'Don't fret, dear.' Meryl's voice was soft and soothing, and she looked at Gloria with all the tenderness of a loving grandmother. 'We'll get you to your girl in time. I'll make sure of it. That rascal will rue the day he meddled with one of my artists!'

'Thank you, Meryl.' Gloria hesitated, unsure if she wanted to ask the question that had been burning in the back of her mind for the last few days. She had been ignoring it so far, but now she was alone with Meryl again, she had to know.

'You've been so good to me, and I am so, so grateful, but I have to ask, why are you doing all this? This has to be above and beyond helping out one of your artists.'

Meryl looked away for a moment as she considered her reply. 'Gloria, have you ever been to the zoo?'

'What?' Gloria frowned at the sudden change in subject, confused. 'What does that have to do with—?'

'Just answer the question, dear.'

'Yes, of course. I used to take Iris when she was little.'

'Well, picture the lions and the tigers at the zoo. They're impressive, of course, but do they have the power and grace that one might expect to see in the wild?'

Gloria shook her head, still not understanding the relevance.

'Of course, they don't. They're confined, defeated. Content enough as their basic needs are met, but their spirit, their soul, is suppressed. They yearn for their freedom.'

'I don't understand.'

'That's what I saw in you, Gloria, from the very moment we met. There's a fire in you. I see it in your paintings. I saw it in your studio, when you forgot about the outside world and allowed yourself to share your passion with me. But you were trapped, dependent on a man who didn't understand or appreciate you. I knew then that I had to help you. I'd do whatever it took to deliver your freedom.'

Gloria grasped Meryl's hand in hers as tears began to well behind her eyes. 'You are an amazing woman, Meryl. I honestly don't know what I did to deserve your friendship.'

Meryl smiled. 'That's your problem, my dear. You don't realise how much you're worth. You have always deserved kindness and respect, and it's about time you let yourself have it.'

Gloria didn't know what to say. She rested her head on Meryl's shoulder, feeling safer and more content than she had in a long time. Meryl squeezed her hand and started off on a story about the shenanigans of the early days of her Amsterdam gallery. Before long, Gloria had drifted off into a peaceful sleep.

◆ —— • ● ◆ • • —— ◆

Gloria awoke to Meryl gently shaking her shoulders.

'Almost there, dear. Wakey wakey!'

Her eyes fluttered open, and she immediately regretted her sleeping position when a dull ache throbbed down the right side of her neck as she lifted her head upright. Her breath caught in her throat as she peered through the window and was greeted by the sight of central Amsterdam, row upon row of narrow, colourful houses casting rainbow reflections in the gleaming canals. She smiled at the assortment of mismatched buildings as they went by, leaning against each other liked old friends, framed beautifully by the array of picturesque bridges. Once upon a time, this had been a routine sight, no more remarkable than her morning bowl of corn flakes. But seeing it again after all these years, it was even more beautiful than she remembered.

It was only mid-morning, but already the city was packed with tourists, snapping away with their cameras and weaving in and out of bars, restaurants and cafés. The whole place was buzzing with life.

Gloria's chest fluttered as the bus approached the Centraal Station. She couldn't wait to get off and immerse herself in the atmosphere of the city again. She knew she had missed living here, but it wasn't until now that she realised just how much. *This* was home. She looked to her right and saw a similar yearning in Meryl's eyes, shining with an almost youthful eagerness.

The bus pulled to a stop, and Meryl continued to stare through the window. The look on her face shifted to one of concern. Excited travellers rose around them and disembarked the bus, but Meryl remained frozen in place.

'Meryl?' Gloria placed a hand on Meryl's shoulder, and she finally blinked and shifted her gaze back to Gloria.

'Quick, let's go. Samuel, come on.' Meryl hurried the group off the bus and, without hesitation, marched them across the street towards the busy centre of the city.

Gloria was confused – Meryl didn't know the way to Alma's. However, she led them on with immense purpose, weaving around tourists and occasionally looking over her shoulder to survey the street behind them. She took a sharp right turn down a side street towards the main shopping district, increasing her pace and pulling Gloria and Samuel along with her.

'Meryl, where are we going?' Samuel asked, frowning at his boss with obvious confusion.

Meryl drew Samuel and Gloria closer to her and spoke in a low voice. 'Don't panic, and for God's sake, don't look, but we're being followed.'

Gloria's chest tightened. *Greg?*

'Who is it?' she asked, her voice coming out as a strangled squeak.

'Some thuggish man. I saw him staring at you through the bus window, Gloria. I think he was waiting for you.'

Gloria's blood ran cold.

Her head was spinning. She didn't know what to think or do. Her body moved numbly as Meryl pulled her along, zigzagging through the narrow streets in a futile attempt to shake off their stalker.

'He's getting closer,' Meryl murmured, subtly peering over one shoulder. 'We have to do something, or he'll be on us any minute.'

'W-what can we do? We can't exactly fight him. He might have a weapon!'

Meryl unhitched her bag from her shoulder and held it firmly in both hands. 'I have an idea. You two keep walking. Don't stop, and I mean that. I'll distract him, whilst you two run. Go anywhere, in any direction, the more random, the better. I'll get in touch and find you when I can.'

Samuel's eyes bulged. 'You can't be serious, Meryl! You could get hurt!'

'I'll be fine. I'm a tough old bird, and I faced scarier guys than this fellow back in the seventies, believe me. Gloria needs to get to her girl, and I'll just slow you both down. Don't argue with me, Samuel, I'm doing it.'

'Meryl,' Gloria grabbed Meryl's arm and stared firmly into her eyes. 'I can't let you do this.'

'Gloria, you're just beginning to come into your own, and I won't let that pig trap you again. You're a strong woman and the mother of a daughter who needs you. Go get her.'

Before Gloria could answer, Meryl twisted out of her grasp and charged towards a tall, bald man dressed all in black. She slammed her bag into his face, sending him tumbling backwards onto the pavement. Gloria and Samuel took their cue and started to run, but ground to a halt as they heard a familiar voice scream out.

Gloria span round to see Meryl sprawled across the pavement, the thug's hand grasped around her ankle where he'd dived at her to prevent her escape. She was already fighting back, buffeting his head into the ground with her bag. She held it down, turning to see Samuel and Gloria, shell-shocked, only a few metres ahead of where she had left them.

'Go!' she screamed, waving her arm wildly as the man started lifting himself onto his knees. 'GO!'

Gloria stood frozen, mind blank, unsure of what to do. She was vaguely aware of Samuel shouting next to her, and numbly stumbled as he pulled her onwards, taking a turn down a narrow side street to get out of view of the attacker. Tears blurred her vision, and she had no idea where she was running, blindly following Samuel as her heart slowly broke into pieces at leaving Meryl behind.

What have we done?

CHAPTER TWENTY-EIGHT

Gloria bent over the sewage grate, her stomach already aching from the retching, but thankfully nothing came up. Samuel rubbed her back, offering her a bottle of water he'd bought from a nearby shop. She took it gladly. The younger man was considerably fitter than Gloria, and before long, he couldn't continue to drag her along with him. The exertion had proven too much, and Gloria had to stop before her body gave out completely. She only wished she could blame the exhaustion for how terrible she felt.

With their escape over, her mind began to refocus, and she was confronted with the last image she had of Meryl, screaming for them to run while her attacker attempted to pull her closer to him. Gloria's stomach clenched, and she sunk to the ground as her legs gave way from under her. They shouldn't have left her behind. Anything could have happened to her, could be happening to her right now, and should the worst happen, it would all be Gloria's fault.

'We-we have to go back...for Meryl,' she wheezed between gulps of air, hands trembling on her lap. Her lungs felt like they were on fire.

For a moment, Samuel was silent, and Gloria wondered if he had even heard her.

'You heard what she said,' he said quietly. 'We have to go on.'

Gloria buried her head in her hands. She'd only known her for a few weeks, but she considered Meryl a good friend. Leaving her behind felt like nothing short of betrayal.

'Do you always just do whatever Meryl says?' she snapped, turning round to stare at Samuel through tear-filled eyes. 'Maybe you need to get a fucking backbone.'

Samuel's face crumpled as Gloria's words cut through him. The hurt was clear in his eyes. *What am I doing?*

'No...I didn't mean that. I'm sorry, Samuel...' Her voice wavered as fresh tears threatened to burst out, and she suppressed a rising sob. 'It's just...Meryl did so much for me, and now she's gone, and we're stuck in the middle of Amsterdam, and I don't know what to do.'

She gave in to the flood of panic and pain, letting it wash over her until she was wracked with sobs she could no longer hold back. Tourists tutted and complained as they had to step around her, but she didn't care. *Let them judge me. What does it matter?*

'We're not necessarily stuck,' Samuel said when Gloria's sobs had quietened down into soft whimpers. 'Meryl had the bag, but I've still got my phone.'

Gloria lifted her head out of her hands and looked up at Samuel. She couldn't believe he was still trying to help after what she had just said to him.

'Come on,' he said, holding out a hand. 'Let's find somewhere, er...less public to figure out where we are and where we need to go.'

Gloria took his hand gratefully, and Samuel pulled her up to her feet. Before either of them could stop it, she had wrapped her arms around him and pulled him into a tight embrace. 'Thank you, Samuel,' she whispered.

In that moment, any residual tension from the previous night evaporated. Samuel was a friend, Gloria knew that, and she was lucky he was here.

◆ ——— • ● ◆ ● • ——— ◆

It didn't take long for them to find somewhere suitable to sit away from prying eyes while they planned their next move. Amsterdam was awash with pubs and cafés, which were already bustling with activity, so they took shelter in the nearest café, a charming little place on a street corner, looking out over a canal. In other cities, the proximity to the canal might have indicated where they were, but not in Amsterdam; there were over one hundred canals and, after years away from the city, they all looked the same to Gloria.

As they stepped inside, it was obvious they would struggle to find a table, as the whole place was packed with tourists recharging before they delved back into sightseeing. The air was abuzz with conversation, multiple languages melding together into one great hum of excitement. Samuel ordered them both a coffee, and once it was ready, they navigated their way back outside to sit at one of the small tables facing the canal. It was a cool morning, so there were thankfully a few spots left, avoided by the less hardy visitors to the city.

Gloria sipped at her coffee as Samuel rummaged in his pockets for his phone, the warm liquid providing a surprising amount of comfort after the events of the morning so far. She peered at the canal, sunlight glinting off its smooth, still surface. Her body ached for the past, when she'd walked over those bridges without a care in the world, sketching the water and the beautiful city which framed it, stood in her own blissful bubble as strangers passed by going about their own business. How she wished she could go back and tell herself to treasure those moments.

'Damn it!' Samuel muttered when he finally unlocked his phone, kicking Gloria out of her daydream.

'What's wrong?' she asked, rising dread already beginning to displace her sweet nostalgia.

'My battery is down to one percent. Meryl had the charger and the power packs, so I didn't worry about it. Plus, we were together, why would I need my phone? I should have charged it on the bus. Idiot!'

Samuel smacked himself in the forehead in frustration. Nevertheless, he made the most of what he had and went straight to work loading up a map and surveying the area around them for landmarks.

'Right, right, I see. I know where we are. Now I just need to – argh!' The screen went black, and he slammed it down on the table, shaking their cups and spilling coffee over everything. 'Oh, crap! Sorry, Gloria, sorry. That was stupid.'

Despite everything, Gloria couldn't help but giggle a little at his flustered apologies. He was a sweet guy. *If I was ten years younger, maybe...*

Samuel looked up at her in confusion.

'I'm sorry.' She smiled, shaking her head. 'How far did you get with the map?'

'I pinpointed our location, so that's something, I suppose. How well do you know the area where Elias's aunt lives?'

Gloria frowned. 'Not very well. We didn't have much money, so we walked everywhere, and Elias always led the way.'

She looked down at the table, feeling utterly useless. A quiet moment passed before Samuel finally spoke.

'Don't worry, we'll think of something.' He rose from the table and placed a gentle hand on Gloria's shoulder. 'Wait here, I'll replace your coffee and then we'll put our heads together and work this out.'

Sat alone at the table, Gloria realised how soothing Samuel's presence had been. Now she was by herself again, anxiety began to bloom in her stomach. When Samuel came back, it would be down to her to find Alma's place. Samuel, Iris, Elias – they would all be relying on her, and the very thought made Gloria's throat tighten with panic. Her eyes scanned the immediate proximity for anything that could distract her from her thoughts, but the laughing tourists enjoying their holiday only darkened her mood.

She opened her handbag and rifled through the forgotten items lurking in the bottom, searching for tissues. The least she could do was help Samuel tidy the mess on the table. Her fingers brushed against something soft, stopping her in her tracks. She lifted the forgotten toy dinosaur out of the bag and held it in the palm of her hand.

I don't need him anymore, so you should take him, so you won't be scared when you're lost.

Daniel had told Gloria he didn't need Rexy anymore, but there she was, lost and frightened yet again, desperately trying to calm her nerves. Did she really possess less courage than a six-year-old child? As she twirled the little toy around in her fingers, a thought struck her. She had spent her entire life running away. She had run away from home, she ran away from the responsibility of being a mum, and now she was running away from Greg. She had been telling herself she had once been confident and carefree, but deep down, she had still been trying to escape, unable to face her past or commit to a future. No wonder she was lost.

It can't go on.

She had to start making things happen for herself instead of following others and hoping they could lead her to salvation. She was in Amsterdam, the city she had lived in and loved for years. It had been her home, until her fear for Iris's future had sent her running into Greg's arms. Regardless, she should be the one leading Samuel through its labyrinthine streets, not the other way around. He was young, and probably more terrified than she was but didn't want to show it. She had to start taking the lead.

By the time Samuel returned with the map, Gloria already had the beginnings of a plan forming in her mind. She may be cut off from the digital world, but she knew this city, and in times like these, you needed to think old school.

It took longer than either of them had expected to find a souvenir shop which actually stocked paper maps – apparently, they were the only people in the city without the use of a mobile phone.

Samuel and Gloria sat together on a bench by the canal and circled their current location on the map. Gloria couldn't remember precisely where Alma's apartment was, but she was a visual learner and knew she'd know the walking route she used to take with Elias. All she needed to do was find her way back to the starting point.

'There,' she said, placing a finger firmly on a street corner. 'There's a coffee shop on that corner where Katie and I used to meet Elias before walking up to Alma's. Once I'm there, I'll know where to go.'

Within a few short minutes, they had plotted their route to the coffee shop and were back on the move. Gloria walked with purpose, pleased to be finally proving herself useful. Her positive mindset seemed to be rubbing off on Samuel, whose head swivelled from side to side to finally take in Amsterdam's beauty, marvelling at its unique charm. He clearly hadn't travelled much himself, and in a way, Gloria envied him. He had his whole life ahead of him, with so much yet to discover.

With their motivation renewed, Samuel and Gloria crossed the city in good time, Samuel taking the role of navigator while Gloria scanned their surroundings for anything familiar. It felt invigorating to be able to live like she had as a younger woman, taking in the sights and sounds of the city and following her own judgement. But it was more than that. For the first time in perhaps her entire life, she was a leader, not a follower. It was scary, but she was doing it. She was actually doing it.

'Right.' Samuel held the map close to his face. 'I believe we walk right to the end of this road, and then it's a left.'

'No.' Gloria surprised them both with her sudden assertion, but she was sure there was a better route. 'No, I know this area, I'm sure. There's a short cut down this side street. Trust me.'

To Gloria's surprise, Samuel didn't question her. He simply nodded and followed her lead as she walked to their immediate left, down a narrow street between two small shops. It was such an inconspicuous opening that most tourists didn't even spot it, and Gloria remembered using it to her advantage when she had wanted to beat the crowds to work. Back then, she'd jumped between a range of part-time jobs to make ends meet, which often meant a mad dash across the city between shifts.

As expected, the side-street was quiet, allowing them to power walk to the opposite end much quicker than if they had been meandering around gawking sight-seers. Gloria loved the hustle and bustle of a thrumming city, but with Iris's safety at stake, she was thankful for any respite from the swarming crowds.

At the end of the street, they emerged into a small square teeming with tourists. Samuel stepped forward before Gloria could stop him, not realising he needed to look both ways before he did so.

'Samuel, wait! That's a—'

It was too late. He had stepped out into a cycle lane, and directly into the path of an oncoming bicycle. The cyclist tried her best to avoid him, but the sudden swerve sent her careering into the pedestrian side of the street, where she crashed into a brick wall. The poor rider was knocked back off her bike and onto the pavement, and Samuel and Gloria both ran to her aid.

While Samuel fussed over her, checking for injuries and apologising profusely, Gloria stood agape, eyes transfixed on the person laid out on the floor in front of them. For a second, she thought her mind might be playing tricks on her, that the stress of the last few days had addled her brain. It would be too good to be true otherwise. But there she was, as clear as day and dressed nowhere near appropriately for a cycle through the city, too distracted by Samuel's attempt at first aid to even notice Gloria.

When Gloria finally found her voice, it came out as a shrill squeak.

'Katie?'

CHAPTER TWENTY-NINE

The two women stared at each other, eyes wide. Gloria's mind raced with so many questions she didn't know where to begin. Katie seemed equally speechless, and it was some time before she hauled herself unsteadily to her feet and threw her arms around her stunned friend.

'Gloria! Oh, thank God you're okay!' Katie squeezed her tightly, either oblivious or uncaring about the small crowd of tourists who had stopped to see what the cause of the commotion was. Samuel quietly ushered them on and pulled Katie's bike to one side so they could have a relatively private conversation.

'What are you doing here?' Gloria asked, pulling back to look at Katie's face. She still didn't quite believe she was there. 'I thought you were in Paris?'

'I was! Hence the, er...' She gestured to her smart black trouser suit, now somewhat ruined by the scrape along the pavement. 'But when I got your message, I got worried. I tried to call you that night, but your phone was completely dead. That's when I really panicked. I cut my trip short and got the first flight here.'

Gloria couldn't believe what she was hearing. 'But...won't you be in trouble with work? You were supposed to be there for weeks.'

Katie shrugged, a small smile playing on her lips. 'Possibly, but I told them it was an emergency, and I'll make it up to them. They won't sack me. They need me too much,' she added with a wink.

'I just...I can't believe you really came!' Tears welled in Gloria's eyes, and they were soon mirrored in Katie's, her eyes shimmering.

'Of course, I came, Glor.' Katie's voice began to tremble. 'I know we've drifted apart a bit ever since...well, over the last few years. But you're like a sister to me, and I couldn't stand by knowing you or Iris could get hurt.'

Ever since Greg. Of course.

Gloria had no words. She pulled Katie in and embraced her tightly, thanking her lucky stars they had found each other on that very first visit to Amsterdam. They had both been lost souls, young and uncertain, desperately seeking out a new life. They'd found solace in one another and promised to look out for each other ever since. As she clutched her friend to her chest, Gloria was wracked with guilt for letting their relationship dwindle in recent years, Greg or no Greg. Katie had deserved better than that.

'Katie,' she mumbled into her friend's thick black hair. 'I'm so sorry we lost touch. I should have made the effort. I didn't—'

'Glor, stop it!' Katie drew back and looked her hard in the face. 'That wasn't your fault. Greg made it perfectly clear I wasn't welcome, and I should have fought against it more instead of letting him push me away. Maybe I could have saved you from this nightmare.'

Gloria frowned. 'Wait...what did Greg say to you?'

Katie smiled and wiped newly forming tears from her eyes. 'Never mind about that now. That man has been allowed to play bully for too long, and we're not going to let him bully your daughter as well. What's the plan? I went to Elias's flat first, but no one was there.'

Gloria's legs almost gave way in relief. At least Elias had been true to his word and taken Iris to safety. 'They should be at Alma's. We were just trying to figure out the way there, and this seemed like a good place to start.'

'"We"? Oh, how rude of me!' Katie turned to Samuel, who had been politely standing with his hands in his pockets while the two friends reunited. Katie held out her hand, suddenly back in business mode. 'I'm Katie Embleton, Gloria's friend. Sorry about the near-miss there!'

Samuel took Katie's hand, smiling awkwardly. 'Don't apologise, really. And nice to meet you, of course! It was all my fault. I'm Samuel, by the way, Samuel Musa. Meryl's assistant.'

'Oh, that's right! Meryl always speaks so highly of you.' Katie flashed him a broad smile, which faded a little as she looked around, her eyebrows knotting in confusion. 'Did Meryl stay behind in London, then?'

There was a long silence as Gloria and Samuel glanced at each other. Gloria felt the heat of shame rise up her neck as she struggled to find the words to explain Meryl's absence.

'No. She ran into issues when we arrived.' Gloria's stomach twisted at the half-truth, but she forced herself to continue. 'I'll explain later.'

Katie's brow creased with concern, but she nodded and asked no further questions. 'Of course, we need to get to Iris and make sure she's okay. Who knows what that slimeball is capable of. Oh, sorry, Gloria,' Katie added, looking a little embarrassed.

'It's fine. I hate that man and have no plans of ever making up with him. Call him whatever you want.'

Katie grinned from ear to ear at that remark, evidently very pleased about Gloria's reformed opinion of her husband.

'Well, I'm sure if we put our heads together, we can quickly find our way to the apartment. Let's go!'

◆———— • ● ◆ ● • ————◆

The going was slower than Gloria would have liked.

With Katie pushing her mangled rental bike alongside them, they travelled much slower than they had as a pair, but with their combined memories, they managed to puzzle together the way to the apartment quicker than Gloria thought she could have managed on her own. In other circumstances it would have been a very pleasant journey, walking with Katie in the summer sun and reminiscing about each landmark they recognised on their way to Alma's, but with each passing recollection, Gloria's anxiety rose. Now she knew what Greg was capable of, she wouldn't be satisfied that Iris was okay until she finally saw her for herself. Katie and Samuel didn't seem as concerned – Elias had whisked her away as soon as possible, after all – but she couldn't shake the uneasy feeling in her stomach, and she grew quieter as they walked on, letting the other two get to know each other as she descended into a sullen silence.

It was with great relief that Gloria recognised Alma's building as soon as they turned onto the correct street. She had been terrified she wouldn't know which one it was, but the striking redbrick building stood out amongst the others.

GLORIA

It was gorgeous, nestled neatly in the middle of a row of similarly narrow townhouses, each with its own unique style and charm. Gloria had always been envious of Alma's place; it was far superior to anything she and Elias could ever have afforded, but Elias's kind-hearted aunt had always welcomed them into her home, no matter the occasion, and Iris had spent many happy weekends in comfort there.

As the building grew closer, Gloria broke into a run, overcome with anticipation now that she would finally see her daughter again. She couldn't wait to hold her in her arms, at last knowing she was safe and out of Greg's clutches. Iris would complain, of course – she had outgrown cuddles years ago – but Gloria didn't care. She would squeeze her so tightly they would have to use a crowbar to separate them again.

When she reached the main door leading into the apartments, Gloria was relieved to find it was unlocked. Without waiting for the others, she let herself in and sprinted up the stairs to the second floor. When Alma's door was in sight, she skidded to a halt, frozen in place. All of her excitement drained from her body, replaced with an icy dread. She felt sick to her stomach.

'Gloria?' Katie called from the floor below, catching up. 'What's wrong? Why have you...oh.'

Gloria didn't turn to look at her friend. She couldn't move. She couldn't speak. Her entire body was numb. She was vaguely aware of Samuel also making his way to the landing, where he stopped, speechless.

Alma's door was ajar, the frame broken where someone had forced their way into the apartment.

We're too late.

CHAPTER THIRTY

It took several minutes before Gloria could bring herself to push open the door and step carefully into the apartment. She could feel her heart pounding in her ears, and her chest rose and fell with breaths so sharp and rapid they were almost painful. The apartment was eerily silent, setting Gloria's nerves on edge. Her eyes slowly scanned the living space in front of her. Everything looked normal. In fact, it was as neat and tidy as ever. Even the sofa cushions were in perfect order. She opened her mouth to call out to Iris, but Katie clamped a hand over it, shaking her head and pointing to the floor ahead of them. Gloria's chest tightened as her gaze followed Katie's finger to a spattering of small red stains on the cream carpet.

Blood.

Panic gripped Gloria's body, and her throat began to tighten. *What has that bastard done? If he has hurt Iris, I will kill him.*

Pushing down her rising fear, she crept onwards, eyes fixed ahead, her entire body tense. Katie gestured towards the dining-room door, the only room which was fully closed off to them. Gloria nodded. If Iris was in this apartment, she was in that room.

She reached a trembling hand to the doorknob, slowly turning it and opening the door less than an inch; just enough to let her peer through. What she saw turned her stomach to lead.

'Oh my god, Elias!' She burst into the room, no longer caring if anyone else was lurking within. 'What have they done to you?'

Elias was sat facing Gloria, tied to a dining chair, and beaten black and blue. His lolling head slowly lifted at the sound of Gloria's voice, and she gasped as she took in the full extent of his injuries. One eye was completely swollen shut, his lip was split, and his usually blond hair was matted with dark blood. He tried to speak, but his voice was muffled by a bloodied rag which had been tied between his teeth. Gloria was relieved to see that they all still seemed to be in his mouth, at least.

She knelt beside him and set to work untying the rag, shouting to Samuel and Katie to find a knife for the cable ties she found holding his wrists behind his back. Now she was closer to him, she could see fresh dark purple bruises blossoming under his white shirt as his chest rose and fell with ragged breaths. He winced with every tug of movement from her hands. Finally, she was able to loosen the knots and remove the cloth from his mouth.

"Gloria...' Elias's voice was coarse and raspy; he had clearly been there a while.

'Samuel, Katie, bring a glass of water, too! My God, Elias, are you okay?' Gloria's blood ran cold as she realised the worst had happened. 'Where's Iris?'

Elias looked down at his knees, and Gloria held her breath, terrified of what would come next. When he looked back up at her, tears glistened in his broken, blue eyes. 'He... he took her, Glor.'

No!

'I'm...I'm so sorry. There was a group of them...they broke in and...I couldn't...I couldn't hold them all off. I...I...' His voice faltered as further tears welled up, threatening to break free. Tracks in the dried blood smeared across his cheeks suggested these weren't the only tears he had shed today.

Gloria felt numb, as if the floor had been pulled away from under her feet and she was falling into the abyss. Iris was gone. They had come all this way, worked so hard to get here, and they were too late. Iris was gone, and Greg was doing God knew what with her.

They had failed.

No, *she* had failed. Iris was the most important thing in her life, and yet she had abandoned her, leaving her vulnerable to attack by the very man she had brought into their lives.

This was all on her.

'I'm...I'm so sorry, Gloria,' Elias breathed, breaking through her bubble of despair. He sounded utterly defeated.

Gloria wrapped her arms around him, laying her head on his chest. 'It's not your fault. It's my fault. This is *all* my fault.'

Fresh tears broke free from her eyes, pouring down her face and raining onto Elias's shirt as violent sobs wracked her entire body. She was vaguely aware of movement behind the chair, and as Elias's strong arms enveloped her, she could only assume Katie and Samuel had managed to free him from his restraints. He squeezed her tight against his chest, stroking her hair with warm, tender hands. She wanted to enjoy the moment, to revel in being back in the sanctuary of his arms, but the overwhelming sense of loss creeping through her body left her unable to feel anything else.

Iris was gone, and it was all because of her.

CHAPTER THIRTY-ONE

'Don't you dare blame yourselves for this.'

Gloria pulled back from Elias to see Katie standing over her, hands on her hips. 'This is all Greg's fault, and I won't let either of you think for a second that you're to blame.'

'But, Katie,' Gloria sniffed, struggling to hold back a sob, 'if I hadn't—'

'No, I won't hear it. You've both done everything you can, and together we *will* get Iris back. This isn't over yet.'

Gloria frowned, willing herself to share Katie's optimism, but what on Earth could they do now? Iris was who knew where, and Greg had a team of cronies on hand to fight off anyone foolish enough try and take her back. Once again, he'd used his money to seize control. He thought he was the big man when, in reality, he was just a spoiled little boy. A coward.

Gloria stood and paced around the dining room. Moving made her feel like she was at least doing something. Her mind was racing, and she needed to calm herself down enough to be able to think straight. Her eyes darted about, desperately hoping to find a clue to steer their next move. Something shiny caught her eye at the other end of the table – a mobile phone.

'Elias, is this yours?' she asked, walking over and holding it up.

'No. I've never seen it before.' He reached for the glass

of water Katie was holding out to him and took a long swig. 'Maybe one of Greg's thugs left it behind by accident. They didn't mess about – I barely had time to react before they'd surrounded me. I suppose I could have knocked the phone out of their hands in the struggle.'

A foreboding sense of dread pulsed through Gloria's body. Greg was always meticulous in his actions. He wouldn't have allowed anything to be left behind unless it was intentional. She tapped the screen, and it came to life – there was no passcode, no security whatsoever, and there, flashing in the middle of an otherwise empty screen, was one new unread message. Before she could stop herself, she opened it, and as she took in what she saw, she almost fell to the ground as her knees buckled and the breath froze in her lungs. She stumbled back onto one of the dining chairs and sat still, staring at the image on the screen.

'Gloria?' Samuel's voice drifted through the periphery of her thoughts, as she became vaguely aware of him standing in the dining room doorway. 'What is it?'

Gloria swallowed and tried to regain her breath. Her heart hammered against her ribs, threatening to punch through her chest.

'A video,' she said quietly, hands trembling as her finger hovered above the "play" button. 'A video of Iris.'

CHAPTER THIRTY-TWO

Samuel, Elias and Katie gathered around Gloria's chair as she held her finger over the screen, unsure if she dare start the video and find out what Greg had done. She already knew he could be violent – he'd proven that with her – but how much of a monster was he? What the hell had he done to her little girl? Her stomach tied itself in knots as she tried to force the worst possible scenarios out of her mind. What ifs wouldn't help now. She had to act.

She glanced up at Elias, who nodded at her with a stern face, his strong jaw clenched. She took a deep breath, her tight chest painfully resisting the flow of air into her lungs, and finally pressed "play".

A shaky image of Iris stared out of the screen, standing still, her bright blue eyes glistening with tears. She hadn't even had the chance to get changed out of her school uniform, although her missing tie and loose, dishevelled hair suggested she'd put up a fight when they'd taken her. Gloria's heart ached at seeing her little girl like that. She appeared to be uninjured at least, and Gloria was surprised to see she didn't look frightened. She looked angry, her pale face set hard as stone.

'Go on, Iris, say it.'

The voice was off-camera, but Gloria's stomach twisted

as she recognised it to be Greg's. Iris didn't respond. She continued to stare directly at the camera, fists clenched by her sides, arms trembling slightly.

'Say it.' Greg's voice was firmer this time, threatening. 'Say it!'

Iris jumped back a little at his raised voice, but she stayed silent, her head shaking slightly in small, quick movements. Her eyes blazed with defiance as she took a few steps back from the camera towards a small, round window, and a surge of pride ran through Gloria as she admired the bravery of her daughter. Iris was already proving to be stronger than her mother.

It was Gloria's turn to jump as Greg lunged from behind the camera and snatched Iris up by the hair. She let out a terrified squeal which cut through Gloria like a knife, and she nearly dropped the phone in terror at what he might do next.

'I'll kill him,' Elias muttered darkly, fists clenched and trembling with rage.

'Come on, now, precious step-daughter.' Greg brought Iris's face close to his, smiling at her with a wicked grin. He yanked her a little higher, and she winced with pain. 'Talk to your mother.'

'M-Mum,' Iris mumbled, glancing away from the camera. 'Th-this is your fault. This is happening because...because of you.'

'Good girl.' Greg turned to face the camera himself, lowering Iris to the ground, but keeping a firm grip on her hair. A flash of anger ran through Gloria's body. She might have let him bully her, but he would pay for torturing her daughter like this.

'You see, Gloria, this didn't need to happen.' He shook

Iris a little more for emphasis, the poor girl whimpering in his grasp. 'I didn't want to hurt anyone. I gave you a chance to come home, and you threw it back in my face. Did you really believe I would let you go so easily?'

Greg's laugh was cold and cruel. 'I tracked your phone, but you probably know that by now. Or maybe you don't. You were never the brightest, were you?'

Bastard.

Gloria's hands trembled so much at the sight of Greg holding her daughter like that, the phone started to shake in her hand. Elias reached down and clasped her free hand with his, squeezing it tight.

Greg pulled Iris up again, and she clenched her teeth to hold back another scream. 'Oh, did you really think I wouldn't keep an eye on my insurance policy here?' He pinched Iris's cheek with mock playfulness, and she batted his hand away, eyes blazing with fury. He began to casually pace about the room, dragging Iris along with him as if she wasn't even there. It looked like a small space, the limited light shining in from the undersized windows revealing outdated floral wallpaper. A living room perhaps.

'Didn't you ever wonder why I was so happy to put your little illegitimate brat through private school? Why I put money in the pockets of your bastard daughter and idiot ex-boyfriend?'

Elias's hand squeezed Gloria's even tighter.

'I did it so I'd know exactly where to find them – and exactly where to keep watch. You were never going to win, Gloria. I've always been in charge, and I always will be. Remember that. Now,' He stopped pacing and brought Iris closer to the camera. 'I'm going to be extremely generous and offer you one last chance. You come back to me, agree to behave yourself, and we forget any of this happened. Iris gets returned safely to Daddy, and we go home together. We can all be one big happy family again. If you don't...well, I'm afraid she stays with me, at least until she's served her purpose. After that, I guess we'll see how well she behaves and how generous I decide to be. Right, sweetheart?'

He moved his face closer to Iris's. She scowled, retracted her head a little and spat across his cheek.

'I always knew you were scum,' she growled through clenched teeth. Gloria gasped, her grip tightening on the phone as she waited for Greg's response.

'Now this,' he said slowly, wiping the saliva from his face with his sleeve, 'is the kind of behaviour I am not willing to tolerate.'

Greg's smirk twisted into a savage sneer as he pulled back his hand and slapped Iris's face with such force that her head rocked backwards, pulling his other hand back as he kept a firm grip on her hair. Gloria flinched, nausea rising in her stomach as she watched her little girl whimpering in his grasp. She felt Elias's hand tighten even more, his breathing growing heavier in her ears. She didn't need to look at him to know he was enraged.

Greg turned back to the camera, that cold, evil grin back on his face. 'Now, to prevent any further ugliness, I suggest we arrange a trade. Mother for daughter, wife for ungrateful stepchild. Daddy over there has my number. I'll give you some time to find this message, and then you *will* call me and arrange a time and place. Somewhere public, where you can't try anything stupid. And, Gloria?' He reached into his jacket and Gloria's entire body clenched as she saw him pull out a sleek, silver pistol.

'No!' she gasped as he pressed the gleaming metal into Iris's temple.

'Don't go involving the police, will you?' Greg's smile was vicious, and his voice dripped with malice. 'If you do, you *will* regret it. Understand? Goodbye, darling. Looking forward to your call.'

The screen froze, and the room grew painfully quiet as they all processed what they had just watched. Gloria gripped the phone with trembling hands, one thought screaming over and over in her head.

He can't do this.

CHAPTER THIRTY-THREE

'Bastard!' Elias shouted, pacing the dining room, hands tangled in his shaggy blond hair. 'I never really liked the guy, but this? This!' He stopped, clenching both his fists, poised as if ready to punch through the door.

Katie strode over to him and placed a gentle hand on his bicep. His head swivelled to stare at her, but as he met her gaze, his face softened, and he lowered his hands.

'So.' Katie pulled Elias over to sit in a chair around the table and gestured for Samuel to do the same. 'How are we going to tackle this?'

'Tackle what?' Samuel asked, lowering himself into a seat. He looked shaken.

'The call to Greg,' Katie said simply. 'We have to discuss what we want to say before we phone him.'

Elias let out a long, exasperated sigh as he dropped into a dining chair, shaking his head. 'Well,' he huffed, 'I guess we need to go in with a suggestion of where to meet, or he's going to try to call *all* the shots.' The hatred was palpable in his voice.

'Good idea.' Katie pulled a pen and notebook out of her handbag and opened it to a fresh page. 'Let's quickly brainstorm which—'

'No.'

Samuel, Katie and Elias turned to look at Gloria in

surprise. She was still staring down at the phone in her hands.

'Gloria?' Katie asked, sounding confused by her friend's sudden interruption.

'I said no,' she replied bluntly, slamming the phone down on the table. She stared across at Katie, jaw fixed. 'We're not doing this.'

'Gloria!' Elias's eyes widened. 'You heard what he said. We have to get Iris back!'

'I know.' Gloria's voice rose, and she met his gaze with equal ferocity. 'Of course, we have to get her. I'm as desperate to save her as you are. But not like this. Not his way.'

'Then what?' Elias's voice rose to match hers, his eyes blazing. 'What do we do? I know you probably don't want to go back, but you can't possibly want to put your own safety above—'

'Of course not!' she screamed, unable to keep the anger out of her voice. 'And how *dare* you even suggest that I would compromise my own child's safety to save myself! Do you really think so little of me, Elias?'

She stared at him, eyes wide with indignation, until his face finally softened and he shook his head, eyes dropping to the table.

'Of course not, Glor. I'm sorry. I...I'm just so worried.' He looked up at her again, baby blue eyes shimmering with tears, and Gloria felt her anger drain from her body.

'I know, it's okay. Neither of us knows how to react to this.' She took a deep breath, trying to clear her mind and calm herself. 'Let's say I go back and do what Greg says, and he *might* stick to his side of the deal and peacefully hand Iris over, but then what? We all live in constant fear of what he might do next? Can we really trust him to leave it at that when we know what he's capable of?'

Gloria sighed and raked a hand through her hair. She took one of Elias's hands in her own, and he looked up at her, an unreadable expression on his face.

'He's been lying to me ever since Day One, Elias, and once again he's sure he can twist me round to his thinking like he always has, but it's not going to work anymore. We have to take a stand.'

Elias's forehead creased with concern, and his voice took on a pleading tone. 'I get it, I do, but we can't put Iris at risk. We just can't.'

'I know, and if I thought handing myself over would keep her safe for good, I'd do it in a heartbeat. But it won't. Not in the long run. You heard what he said – "I've always been in charge, and I always will be". He won't leave it here, Elias! She'll be in danger forever, with Greg breathing down her neck for the rest of her life, and I won't let that happen. I just won't!'

'Right.' Katie rose from the table, holding a palm up to both of them, eyes begging for resolution. 'So, saying we *don't* follow Greg's orders, what do we do?'

Gloria paused for a moment, Greg's threats echoing in her head.

Think. Think.

'To start off,' she began slowly, an idea forming in her mind, 'we figure out where they are.'

'And how the hell are we supposed to do that, Glor?' Elias threw up his hands. 'That room was so fucking generic, they could have been anywhere in Amsterdam.'

Gloria stared down at the phone, still lying on the table. There had to be something in that video they could use.

But what?

She couldn't let her mind be overcome with panic. That's exactly what Greg wanted, what he'd always used to control her. She had to think. Her finger twitched as she thought about replaying the video, but she couldn't do it. She couldn't watch Iris go through that again. She would just have to use what she could remember.

Think.

It starts with Iris. She backs off towards the wall – was it a wall? There was a window...

'That's it.' She spoke before the idea had fully crystallised in her mind, but as her thoughts raced, she grew even more certain that she was right. 'The window.'

◆———— • ● ◆ ● • ———— ◆

'Look.' Gloria paused the video just before Greg emerged from off-camera. 'You can't really see this window until Iris backs up to it.'

Elias, Katie and Samuel were once more gathered around Gloria's chair, eyes fixed on the small screen in her hands.

Samuel sounded confused. 'Well, she's scared of Greg, so she was backing off from him, right?'

Gloria looked over her shoulder at Elias, who was nervously picking at his nails. He'd always been an open book, unable to hide his emotions. She wished she'd appreciated that more when they were together. Elias never kept secrets from her.

'Elias, when has Iris ever been scared of anyone?'

'Well, never.' He looked at Gloria, eyes locking onto hers. 'But this is different. She's under threat, of course she's scared.'

'Maybe. But I think it's something else. Look at the window.' Everyone leaned in closer to get a clear look at the screen. 'Where have you seen windows like that in Amsterdam?'

There was a moment of silence as they each considered the still image. The longer it went on, the more sure Gloria was that she was on to something. Elias was the first to break the silence.

'Nowhere I've been. It's round – almost all of the buildings have square windows. At least, I think so.'

'I think...' Katie's voice was quiet and uncertain. 'I think I might have seen one building like that. I'm struggling to place it, though.'

'I have an idea.' Gloria held up the phone. 'How do we zoom in on this?'

Samuel took the device from her and used his fingers to enlarge the still image.

'Focus on the window. Can we see what's out there?'

Samuel moved the image to centre the window on the screen. Beyond the round frame, there was a blurry image of greenery. They may have been unclear, but the shapes were unmistakable: grass, trees, flowers. Gloria let out a sudden, high-pitched laugh. She was right!

Elias looked down at her, confusion painted across his face. 'What is it?'

Gloria shook her head in disbelief.

'I think I know where it is.'

CHAPTER THIRTY-FOUR

'I really don't see how this is related.'

'Katie, please, just find the photos you sent through to Meryl.'

'Okay, okay.' Katie sighed as she waited for Elias's old laptop to whir into life. He gave it to Alma several years ago as an additional way to reach the rest of their family back in Sweden, but Gloria doubted she had ever actually used it. Alma had always preferred to socialise in person, and was forever organising face to face reunions with distant family and friends. No doubt that was where she was now.

Thank God.

Every muscle in Gloria's body tensed as the outdated machine slowly booted up; this wasn't going to be quick. With each second that passed, she imagined more and more terrible scenarios that Iris could be in at this very moment, with Gloria powerless to stop them. Acid rose up her throat and she struggled to swallow it back down. She couldn't breathe.

'I-I need some water,' she mumbled, and staggered out of the dining room into the kitchen.

Her stomach ached as she retched over the sink, drawing up nothing but acrid, yellow bile. She felt hollow, as if the pain and suffering she had been desperately trying to repress all day was finally surfacing, leaving behind an empty shell. Exhaustion melted over her body, and she wanted nothing more than to sleep, but she couldn't. Not until Iris was safe.

'You should drink something.'

Gloria jumped and turned to see Samuel standing next to her, warm, brown eyes full of sympathy.

'I'm fine,' she croaked, feeling anything but.

'Gloria,' he reached out and placed a soft hand on her arm, and she noticed the absence of the electricity she had experienced the previous night. Something was different. 'You haven't had anything to eat all day, and you're clearly shattered. You need to look after yourself.'

She rubbed her eyes and fought back the tears which threatened to escape. 'I need to find Iris. That's all that matters.'

'You'll be no good to her if you're exhausted.' Samuel grabbed a glass from the nearest cupboard and reached behind Gloria to fill it with water from the tap above the sink. He placed it into her hand. 'Start with this. Please, let me help you.'

She couldn't help but smile. Samuel barely knew her, and yet he had shown her nothing but kindness in the short time they'd spent together. She raised the glass to her lips, and he beamed as she took a tentative mouthful. The cold liquid soothed the burning in her throat, but did nothing to still her nerves. Her eyes were drawn back to the dining room, where Katie still sat staring narrow-eyed at the laptop screen while Elias paced the room in frustration. He had always been an emotional man, and he looked as if he was about to burst. Whether it was with rage or anxiety, she couldn't tell. Most likely both.

'You still love him, don't you?'

The question caught Gloria off-guard, and she drew her attention back to Samuel. His smile had faded.

'What?' She frowned at him, but he didn't respond, waiting for her answer. 'He's Iris's dad, so of course there are feelings there. But it isn't romantic, not anymore.'

Samuel raised an eyebrow, and a small smile reappeared on his lips. 'It's okay, Gloria, really.' His smile widened a little, but a tinge of sadness lingered in his eyes. 'We'll always have the Sky Lounge, I suppose.'

With that, he turned away to rummage in another cupboard, leaving Gloria confused, still clutching her half-empty glass. She shook her head; she was too tired to think, and they had work to do. She could worry about this later. Samuel eventually turned back around, waving an unopened bag of *stroopwafels*. He opened it and handed it to Gloria, his firm expressing telling her she didn't have a choice – she had to eat something. A wave of guilt washed over her as she took the bag from him and realised they were chocolate flavour – Iris's favourite.

The first cookie had barely touched her tongue when they were interrupted by Katie shouting from the dining room.

'Gloria! I've found them!'

CHAPTER THIRTY-FIVE

'These are the ones,' Katie pointed at an array of files on the screen. 'All the photos I snapped when we were trying to get your paintings sold around here. But how will they help?'

'I'm hoping I can show you in a minute,' Gloria said, sliding the laptop in front of her to get a closer look at the images. Various scenes of Amsterdam flashed on the screen, everything from parks to canals to rows of picturesque houses. 'There's one I remember...a-ha!'

Gloria moved the laptop to the middle of the table so everyone could get a good view of the image she had settled on. 'What do you see?'

Katie, Elias and Samuel leaned in to get a better look.

'Oh my God! Gloria, is that it?'

Katie pressed her finger on the screen, her perfectly manicured nail pointing towards a dark-brick townhouse. There was one noticeable feature which made it stand out from the ones which surrounded it: circular windows.

'Gloria, you are a genius!' Elias swept Gloria out of her chair and planted a forceful kiss on her lips. A slight flutter passed through her stomach – she had forgotten how passionate Elias could be. He drew back, his blue eyes bright with fresh hope.

Gloria felt a new heat crawl across her cheeks.

Come on, it's only Elias. No need to be flustered.

'How did you remember painting this?'

'It wasn't until I saw the green through the window that I was sure. The house is across from the Sarphatipark. Remember that place?' She shook her head at Elias's blank expression – he had never had a good memory. 'It was the closest park to that pokey little flat we first got together, so I used to go there often between shifts. One day, I noticed the unusual windows, so I sketched the house and went back later to paint a landscape there.'

'Wait.' Elias stared off to the side, deep in thought. 'Is that the little park in De Pijp? The one with the lake?'

'Yes, why?'

Elias let out a small chuckle and shook his head. 'I used to take Iris there! Before we moved to the bigger apartment, she used to love wandering around the little lake and looking at all the houses. Do you...do you think she knew? When she was being filmed?'

Gloria felt a surge of pride – her daughter was smarter than she had realised.

'Clever girl!' Katie clapped her hands in delight. 'This is amazing! We know where they are. Now what?'

Gloria braced herself for a backlash. She had got them on board so far, but the next stage of her rapidly evolving plan might be a step too far.

'We call the police.'

◆ —— • ● ◆ ● • —— ◆

'No, we're not doing it. I won't do it.'

Elias paced the dining room, voice rising as he continued his objections. Gloria watched him as calmly as she could, waiting for his temper to simmer. 'You heard what he said, Gloria! He'll hurt Iris. He's got a fucking gun! I can't believe you're even suggesting this!'

'I don't think he will.' She kept her voice quiet but firm.

'You don't *think*? That's all you're going with? Gloria, this is our daughter!'

'I know, Elias, but will you just calm down for five seconds so we can talk about this rationally?'

Elias's eyes continued to bulge, but he took a deep breath and sat across from Gloria, hands tightly laced on the table in front of him. 'Okay. Go on.'

'Two things. One, we can all agree that Greg is a liar, right?' Gloria glanced around the table to see each person nodding in turn. 'He also thinks I'll believe anything he says. He's sure he's still got a hold over me, and that's why he's using an empty threat to make us do what he says.'

'But how do you know—?'

'Two,' Gloria continued, speaking over Elias's interruption, 'Iris is just as important and useful to him as I am. He called her his "insurance policy" for a reason, Elias. He wouldn't risk losing us both. We're too valuable to him.'

Gloria couldn't help but cringe; she hated speaking about herself and Iris like that. Like they were commodities to be traded and bartered for.

Elias didn't look convinced, but his face softened, and he

relaxed his hands. His eyes dropped as he let out a quiet sigh. Gloria took one of his hands in hers and lifted his chin so she could meet his gaze.

'I'm not taking Iris's safety lightly here, I promise. I love her more than anything else in the world. I know it might not always seem that way, but I do, and I'd do anything to make sure she's safe. And that's why we need to be smart about this. With all the will in the world, we can't do this alone.'

Gloria stared deeply into Elias's eyes, imploring him to understand. He had been there from the beginning. He knew how much she had feared for Iris's wellbeing, how she was wracked with worry that her baby wouldn't have a good start in life. It had almost destroyed her and had catalysed the end of their relationship. To this day, she still carried the guilt of what she had put him through, and had never blamed him for breaking up with her.

'I know I've panicked in the past, but I'm thinking clearly now, maybe more clearly than I ever have before. I know I probably don't deserve it after all the mistakes I've made, but I need you to trust me now. Not for me; for Iris.'

Elias squeezed Gloria's hand and closed his eyes. After several long moments, they opened and were fixed with a new look of calm resolve. He nodded, a small smile creasing his lips, and Gloria let out a breath of relief. 'Okay, Gloria. I trust you.'

'Thank you.' She leaned forward and wrapped her arms around his neck, taking in his woody, comforting scent. Her stomach fluttered as she realised how much she had missed it. How she wished she could melt into his arms and forget what was happening around her.

There was no time for that, though. They had to save Iris.

She drew back, becoming painfully aware of Samuel and

GLORIA

Katie sat silently watching them. Katie was grinning in that mischievous way of hers, and Gloria fixed her with a firm stare to remind her of the severity of their situation.

'So,' Gloria said, coughing a little to further break the silence, 'first things first. Katie, do we still have friends on the force?'

CHAPTER THIRTY-SIX

Gloria drummed her fingers on the table, nerves prickling the skin all over her body. Back at the apartment, she'd been certain this would work, but as the waiting went on, doubt began to creep back in.

No. I'm doing the right thing for Iris. No more doubting myself. That's what he wants.

She rubbed her eyes, not caring if her makeup got smudged. She was already exhausted, they all were, but they had to press on. They couldn't risk Greg moving Iris to a new location and losing their only lead. Every minute they lost put Iris at greater risk.

She was glad of the distraction when Katie finally returned from the bar, weaving through the throng of other customers with a glass of gin and tonic in each hand.

'I thought a little Dutch courage wouldn't go amiss.'

Gloria took the drink gratefully, knocking back half of it in one swallow. 'He will come, right? It's been so long.'

'He'll be here, Gloria, he promised. Lucky for us, he's been promoted to a big shot in the *Politie* now and can easily break away to come and meet us.' She frowned and looked towards the entrance. 'Where are the guys?'

Gloria nodded towards the far side of the bar, where crowded tables of babbling tourists obscured half of the room. 'I told them to sit out of sight so we can talk to Hendrick alone. You know how funny he is about strange men.'

Hendrick was a kind-hearted man, but he definitely preferred the company of women, which Gloria and Katie had benefited greatly from when they were new to the city.

'Ha! You're right there. I'm sure Elias is keeping a keen eye on us, wherever he is.'

Gloria nodded – Elias had not been happy about being kept out of this meeting, so he would almost certainly be close by, watching their every move. *I wish he would trust me*, she thought bitterly, although she knew she probably didn't deserve it with her track record. She was doing the right thing this time, though, she was sure of it.

Gloria had only agreed for Elias to come to the bar because she knew it would get Samuel out of the apartment; he couldn't get in contact with Meryl, no matter how much he tried, and was worried sick. Gloria told herself it was probably because Meryl's phone had been broken in the scuffle with Greg's thug, but a tight knot in her stomach warned her of other possibilities. A fresh wave of guilt flooded her body, but she had to focus on saving Iris. If they didn't get her back, Meryl's sacrifice would have been for nothing. They would scour the city for her as soon as Iris was safe; Gloria would search all night if she had to.

'Well, if it isn't my Golden Girls!'

They could hear him before they could see him. Hendrick may have grown older, but his voice had the same rich, booming tone as it had had over a decade ago. It rose above the noise of the busy bar, and Gloria noticed several heads swivelling around from neighbouring tables to observe this high-volume newcomer as he strolled through the crowd, his plump, ruddy face beaming.

'Hendrick!' Katie jumped up to embrace their old friend, and Gloria followed suit. Hendrick's affability hadn't waned over the years, and he squeezed her tight as they reunited. He sat down next to Katie, his broad shoulders almost pushing her into the side of the booth.

Hendrick had always been a formidable man, but years at the top of the Amsterdam Police Corps had clearly taken their toll. His once thick head of brunette hair had thinned to almost baldness, and his bright, brown eyes had begun to sink into his face. *He looks tired.*

'Well.' He clapped his hands together, eyeing each of the women in turn. 'What's going on? Katie sounded uncharacteristically serious on her call.'

Gloria took a deep breath. *Where do I start?*

'It's Iris,' she blurted out, deciding to be as straightforward with her old friend as possible. 'She's in trouble.'

'Oh, Iris! Such a lovely little girl. How old must she be now? Ten? Twelve?'

'Almost sixteen.'

'My God! Where have the years gone? It feels like only yesterday I was pulling *you* out of trouble after those late shifts in the club.'

'Hendrick.' Gloria locked eyes with his. 'This isn't just a bit of trouble with the boys like the old days. This is really serious. She's in danger, and we need your help.'

Hendrick's eyes hardened, and his jovial expression shifted to one of purpose. She had seen this look before, and it meant business. He reached into his jacket and pulled out a small notebook and pen.

'Tell me everything.'

Hendrick's eyes grew wider by the second as Gloria gave him a brief rundown of their situation. When she had finished, they were practically bulging out of a face which had grown crimson with anger.

'And you're quite certain you know where he's keeping her?'

'Yes. The house across from the Sarphatipark, I'm sure of it.' She reached across the table and took his hand in hers, her eyes boring into his as she implored him to help. 'We can't do this alone, Hendrick. Greg is dangerous. We need your help.'

He sat back and considered this for a moment, running a hand over what was left of his hair as he reviewed the notes he'd taken. Gloria waited for his response with rising anxiety, her tight chest threatening to cut off her air supply completely.

Finally, he reached across the table and took Gloria's hand in his. 'Girls, it's been years since that first night I walked you home, and I know you probably see me as a funny old man now. But I promised I'd look after you then, and I meant it. That promise extends to your baby girl.'

Gloria's heart leapt. 'So you'll help us?'

Hendrick closed his notebook, returned it to his pocket, and got up from the table, eyes blazing. 'Yes. We will bring this monster to justice. That is my new promise.'

GLORIA

Gloria struggled to breathe as the car made its way closer to De Pijp. Hendrick had been confident in his plan, and even Elias had been brought around to it eventually, but now it was in motion, uncertainty began to stir in Gloria's chest. Hendrick was good at his job. He'd been promoted to the highest rank after all, and he had been good to them in the past. But this was much more serious than the scrapes she and Katie had got into when they were younger.

That wasn't fair; she knew she had a lot to thank Hendrick for. In fact, she wasn't sure how she would have survived those first couple of years in Amsterdam without his help. She had been frightened the night she met him, alone and unsure how to carry on. Staring out through the car window as the coming twilight enveloped the city, she remembered it clearly.

She had been shivering under the shelter of a closed shop's doorway while the cold rain lashed against the pavement, not knowing where to go or what to do next. The darkness of the coming night was sweeping down the street when a broad-shouldered young man had found her and asked for her name in Dutch. Of course, she didn't understand him and had feared the worst as he reached a hand out to touch her shoulder. She didn't know he was, in fact, a concerned policeman, and he wanted to help her.

And he had helped her, so very much. He had found her a safe place to stay, away from the streets, where she could start her new life, and suggested a few places she could find work. When Katie had arrived on the scene a few months later, he took her under his wing also, and she and Gloria became inseparable. Hendrick continued to look out for them both, insisting on walking them home after their late work shifts to make sure they made it back to their hostel without being accosted by the local low-lives. He may have had the manner of an overfriendly uncle, but he had been a God-send, and Gloria probably owed him her life.

Elias reached over from his seat beside Gloria and squeezed her hand. His touch was warm and reassuring, and she was relieved when he didn't take his hand back. He rubbed his thumb over the back of her hand, and the hairs on her arms stood on end. Elias could be bullish, but he was caring and passionate, with a fire inside him that Gloria hadn't experienced with anyone else since. She had railed against it in the past, calling him stubborn, pig-headed and reckless, when in reality, it had been love. She realised that now.

'You remember what you need to do?' Elias said softly, turning worried eyes to Gloria.

'Yes.' Gloria took the deepest breath her constricted chest would allow. 'I can do this, Elias.'

He smiled, his eyes glistening. 'I know you can.'

He leaned further in and planted a soft kiss on her forehead, running his strong fingers through her hair. She closed her eyes, drawing from the comfort of his lips, drinking in the warmth of his touch. She let out a soft sigh as he drew back, not wanting the moment to end.

I love you.

She wanted to say it, but the words wouldn't come. It was too late, she realised with an ache in her heart. She had done too much damage.

GLORIA

'We're here,' the officer driving the car announced abruptly, as they pulled up to a stop outside the park. 'Are you ready, miss?'

Gloria bit her bottom lip and looked out of the window, towards the house. Her daughter was in there, with *him*. Her stomach clenched, but she was ready.

'Yes. Let's do it.'

CHAPTER THIRTY-SEVEN

Gloria's fist trembled slightly as she raised it and knocked on the narrow wooden door. She resisted the urge to look back over her shoulder at Elias, waiting on the opposite side of the road, obscured by the growing darkness of the evening. She took a deep breath.

Confident. You have to look confident.

She stepped back to the edge of the pavement, as far as she could get from the door whilst staying on this side of the road.

You can come to me this time, you bastard.

There wasn't a response, and Gloria resisted the urge to panic. This *had* to be the right address, she was certain of it. At least, she had been certain back at Alma's apartment. As time slowly dragged onwards, nagging doubts threatened to creep in. She tried to picture the landscape she had painted in her mind, but it was already getting fuzzy. Those windows were the same ones. They had to be.

After several long minutes, she finally saw movement through the window in the door, and she allowed herself to hope.

He has to come. He needs me, he said so himself.

The seconds passed by painfully slowly as two figures appeared through the frosted glass, making their way towards the door. It was difficult to tell from their blurred outlines, but Gloria thought she could see a man and a woman; Greg and Iris. She prepared herself for the showdown.

Please, please, let her be okay.

Finally, she heard the sounds of heavy locks being slid open on the other side of the door. Gloria held her breath. The moment had finally arrived – she was going to see her daughter again.

The door opened, and Gloria gasped as she laid eyes on Iris at last. The fiery, defiant teenager from the video had withered into a pale, scared little girl. Her eyes were swollen and bloodshot from tears, and Gloria's fists clenched as she spotted a broken lip. *I'll kill him*, she thought, but forced her face to remain neutral. Greg stood directly behind Iris, lurking in the partial shadow of the doorway. To Gloria's disappointment, he didn't look at all shocked that she had tracked him down. In fact, his expression was one of knowing victory, the hunter who had finally cornered the vixen.

We'll see about that.

'I'm here Greg, just like you asked,' she called out, straining to minimise the quiver of fear in her voice. 'Now let Iris go.'

Iris jerked to run forward, but was halted by something behind her arm. Greg's grin widened, splitting his villainous face, and he raised his arm into the air. As if she was his marionette puppet, Iris copied his action exactly, and Gloria's breath caught in her throat as she spotted the handcuffs.

'What is this?' she asked, a touch of anger creeping into her voice. 'You said if I came back, she could go!'

'And that's still the case.' Greg looked pleased with himself, and Gloria's heart fluttered with dread. 'But did you really expect me to just let her go running off into Daddy's arms whilst you're stood in the street, free as a bird? Give me some credit, please.'

A niggle of doubt began to gnaw at Gloria; this hadn't been part of the plan.

Stay strong. Keep going.

'Okay. Bring her here, and we'll trade places.'

Greg let out a short, sharp laugh, sending a chill down Gloria's spine.

He's suspicious. He knows we've planned something.

'And let you ambush me with whichever friends you decided to bring with you?' Greg laughed, shaking his head. 'No. We do this on my terms, or not at all. You come to me. Then we do the swap. You seem to forget, I only need *one* of you.'

'Gloria! Don't—'

'Elias, it's okay.' She held out her hand to signal for him not to approach. *Don't ruin this.* 'We agreed to trade, so we'll trade. Greg, you'd better let her go. You promised.'

'Would I lie to you?'

Greg's grin was nothing short of devilish. Nevertheless, Gloria started to walk forwards. Their preference had been to draw Greg out to them, so Hendrick's officers could move in, but they'd have been fools to not have a plan B. She moved as slowly as she could without drawing too much suspicion, hoping it gave time for the other officers to close in on the house, unseen.

As Gloria approached, Iris's wide eyes locked onto hers, and she thought she detected a subtle shaking of her head.

Don't worry, sweetheart, I'm getting you out of here.

Greg held out his handcuffed hand, and Gloria had to repress a shudder as she took it. Her skin crawled at his touch, and she wanted nothing more than to turn and run and escape this villain she had brought into her family. *It's almost over,* she told herself. *Just hang on a little bit longer.*

Greg closed his fingers around hers in an iron grip, twisting her hand painfully as he jerked her around and pulled her back against his body. Gloria's vision swam as she tried to understand what was happening, time seeming to slow. A flash of silver moved through her peripheral vision, and she was vaguely aware of the sound of a high-pitched scream erupting from her left. She stiffened as a cold, hard piece of metal pressed into the small of her back, frozen with pure terror. Her stomach twisted as she felt Greg's warm, moist breath whisper into her ear.

'My terms, or not at all.'

Gloria's sight settled into place as she saw Elias striding towards her, face distorted with rage.

'I wouldn't come any closer if I were you, big guy,' Greg announced, twisting Gloria so Elias could catch a glimpse of the gun. His anger didn't subside, but it was enough to halt him in his tracks.

'Give me back my daughter, you big-headed prick.'

'Of course.' Greg's false geniality made Gloria's skin crawl. 'Gloria, the key to the handcuffs is in my top pocket. Take it out.'

She did as Greg asked, using her free hand to fumble in the pocket of his shirt until her trembling fingers found the small metal key. She slowly held it up in front her, hands shaking.

'Good girl. Now unlock her hand and her hand only.'

Gloria complied, resisting the rising urge to fight back, to struggle, to scream, to do anything other than play into the hands of her vile husband.

GLORIA

How did I ever love him?

She turned to Iris, who stood horror-struck at her side, eyes bulging with fear. Gloria took the opportunity to bring her closer and kissed her on the top of her head.

'Don't worry,' she whispered. 'It'll be okay, I promise.'

'Gloria!' Greg barked, and she jumped, almost dropping the key. 'Open it! Quickly, no messing about.'

It took a few attempts before Gloria's shaking hand navigated the key into the lock. As she slid open the cuff from around Iris's wrist, she leaned in close and whispered, 'Run!'

Iris didn't hesitate, sprinting forwards into Elias's arms and releasing furious sobs into her father's chest. Elias soon broke down himself, holding her close as quiet tears streamed into her hair. Gloria yearned to join them, to have her child safe in her arms. To be a family again. Her feet itched to run, but the cold pressure of the gun kept her frozen in place.

'Pathetic.' Greg's voice was cold, unfeeling.

With his free hand no longer bound to Iris, he ran his fingers up Gloria's spine, sending goosebumps rippling over her skin. She opened her mouth to question his actions but was silenced as he closed his fingers around the collar of her jacket and yanked it down, pulling her arms back painfully in the process.

'What are you doing?' she called out as he pulled off the jacket and threw it behind him, into the house. He started running a rough hand over her torso, and Gloria had to resist the impulse to cringe at his touch.

Greg ignored her until he was satisfied, eventually letting out a low chuckle. 'It seems I was giving you too much credit, darling. No wires, no microphone, no phone, nothing. Or perhaps you're finally learning to behave.'

That's what you think.

'Now,' he continued, his voice hardening. 'put the key back in my pocket and put the cuff around your wrist.'

'What?' Gloria's stomach flipped, dread flooding her body. 'Why?'

Greg laughed, and Gloria cringed as his breath caressed the back of her neck. 'You lost your privileges when you ran out on me.'

Gloria's heart sank.

This wasn't supposed to happen.

Her mind raced, but she couldn't think of anything else she could do. She had to follow Greg's instructions and hope for another chance for Hendrick's men to move in. Elias looked up, poised, as if ready to charge in and prevent her from being held captive. She shook her head with the slightest of movement, hoping he would stay back and keep Iris away from the house and out of Greg's clutches. That's what mattered now.

She returned the key to Greg's pocket, dropping it into place to minimise contact with his evil body. A surge of energy ran through her, and for one reckless second, she was going to run. She would throw her head back into his and lurch forward into freedom. She could risk it – she would be willing to gamble with her own safety if it guaranteed a life liberated from the monster breathing down her neck.

But it isn't just my safety.

Iris was right there, and so was Elias. If she made a break for it, she wouldn't only be putting her own life in danger, but also theirs. She had crossed the North Sea to reach Amsterdam and ensure Iris was safe, and she couldn't jeopardise that now. Iris's safety was more important than Gloria's ever could be.

She frowned as she closed the metal ring around her own

wrist, cold anxiety creeping through her body as the handcuff clicked, tying her to Greg.

'Done,' she said coldly, continuing to stare straight ahead. 'Now can we lose the gun?'

'Once we're inside.' Greg raised his voice, directing his attention to Iris. 'Let's hope Mummy behaves herself from now on, so there'll be no more problems. And remember – I've got my eye on you, sweetheart. That's the difference between me and you, Elias. I always get what I want.'

With that, he backed into building, pulling Gloria after him. She just had time to glimpse the fresh tears pouring down her daughter's face before the door slammed shut behind her.

CHAPTER THIRTY-EIGHT

Gloria stumbled as Greg pushed her up a steep staircase, his pistol pressed sharply into the small of her back. The short, surly man who had closed the door behind them lingered to stand guard, presumably to keep watch for a rebellion from Elias whilst Greg escorted her to whichever corner of the house he planned to lock her away in.

'Do you really think things can go back to normal, Greg?' she asked as she staggered onto a narrow landing. The carpet was so thick with dust, she couldn't tell what colour it was supposed to be, and the old-fashioned patterned wallpaper was terribly discoloured and peeling in places. The whole place looked like it had been uninhabited for months, perhaps even years.

'Of course not, you idiotic woman.' Greg laughed, pushing her down the corridor. The house was incredibly narrow, and the walls seemed to press together from either side of her. 'Now everything's out in the open, there's no need to keep you sweet anymore. You could have enjoyed the high life, Gloria, but you've ruined all that now. You can expect to be very bored once we're home. Your "studio" is being dismantled as we speak. I'm not wasting a single penny on you anymore.'

Greg pulled Gloria to a sudden stop near the end of the

corridor at a narrow blue door, causing her to jerk backwards and almost collide with her captor. She turned to face him and surveyed his face. Without the mask of false love he'd been deceiving her with all these years, his features were sharp and cruel, his twisted sneer giving him an almost inhuman appearance. Gloria couldn't believe she had ever found him attractive. How weak had she been to allow this beast to pull her away from her family, all on false promises of a life of magic and romance?

Never again.

'You disgust me,' she spat, meeting his cold gaze with her own.

Greg grabbed the back of her neck with a grip so hard it sent pain shooting up the back of her head, and brought her face an inch away from his. She shrank away from his hot, heavy breath, making no attempt to hide her revulsion. 'The feeling is mutual.'

He pushed open the door and dragged Gloria into a dark, scantily furnished bedroom. The dust was even thicker here, although several streaks and sets of footprints on the old wooden floor suggested a flurry of recent movement. Greg hauled her to a large radiator against the wall, its white paint yellowing and flaking onto the floor.

'Unlock my wrist, quickly. No funny business.'

Wincing through the pain now creeping down her spine, Gloria complied, freeing Greg's hand. He released his grip on her, throwing her forwards onto the floor as he did so. She only just managed to bring her hands up in time to stop her face from slamming into the hard wood, but could do nothing to prevent her knees from colliding with the floorboards, sending a sharp pain shooting up both legs.

Before she could gather herself, Greg slipped the loose cuff through the radiator and locked it tight.

'You'd better get comfortable,' he said, drawing himself up and smoothing out his jacket. 'You'll be there a while. I'll be back for you later.'

He stalked off through the doorway and slammed the door behind him, leaving Gloria in near-complete darkness, punctured only by a crack of light creeping out from between a tiny gap in the old, moth-eaten curtains. As she surveyed the room, she wondered how Greg had accessed this old, decrepit house. *Maybe he's had it on standby for years, in case I woke up one day and decided to leave him.* The thought made her blood run cold.

She shifted her focus to her hand, trapped within the metal handcuff. She thanked her lucky stars Greg hadn't bothered to check it very well, and so hadn't noticed the generous space she'd left around her wrist. She only hoped it was enough.

She slowly pulled her hand back into the opening of the handcuff, testing how far she could get it before it grew uncomfortable. Even with the slack she'd given herself, it was going to be difficult, and most likely painful. She took a deep breath and pulled, trying her best to wrench her hand through the cuff. She made it only halfway before the pain was too much, and she released her hand, defeated.

'Shit!' She kicked the radiator, and a loud ringing reverberated through the room. 'Come on, come on, come on!'

She was about to try again when a soft moan erupted from the corner of the room. She froze, her pulse racing. Turning her head slowly, she listened out to identify the source of the noise. She had assumed the room was empty, but as she stared into the darkness, Gloria realised she wasn't alone. A second moan seemed to emanate from what seemed to be a pile of blankets on a bed in the far corner of the room, silhouetted in the narrow shaft of light creeping in from the window.

'Stay back!' Gloria shouted, her faux confidence betrayed by a distinct tremble of fear in her voice. 'I'm warning you!'

'Gloria?'

It was several seconds before recognition finally came. Gloria's stomach flipped with a sickly mix of hope and dread. 'Meryl? Is that you?'

The blankets unravelled and, as Gloria's eyes adjusted to the darkness, she saw them melt into the shape of the art dealer, looking a little bruised and dishevelled, but otherwise in good health. Gloria's heart soared at seeing her friend again, and knowing she was safe and well lifted a weight from her shoulders she had been suppressing all day. The realisation sent a pang of guilt through her, but she reminded herself it had all been for Iris. When Meryl's dazed eyes finally settled on Gloria, a small smile came to her lips.

'It's so good to see you.' Meryl's eyes widened, and her smile dissolved into an uncertain frown. 'Wait, does that mean...? Is Iris out?'

'Yes, yes, she's outside with Elias. All thanks to you, and Samuel and Katie. It's wonderful to see you too, and...I'm so sorry, Meryl. For leaving you behind.'

Momentarily forgetting her predicament, Gloria moved towards her friend, but her shoulder was yanked back as the handcuff clanged against the metal radiator.

Damn it!

'What you did, Meryl...' She felt tears welling behind her eyes but managed to hold them back. 'It was amazing.'

Meryl didn't say anything, but she didn't need to; her smile said everything.

'They didn't hurt you did they? Why did they bring you here?'

Meryl winced as she sat up straighter. 'A little, but it's just superficial. That brute from the bus stop wasn't gentle when he threw me off him, but they haven't laid a finger on me since I got here. I think that husband of yours wanted me as some sort of backup hostage in case things took a turn for the worse.'

Gloria's stomach turned to ice as she imagined Greg threatening Meryl – or worse, hurting her. He was continuing to shock her with his escalating aggression, and she had no doubt in her mind there was more to come, for both of them.

We have to get out of here.

Gloria cocked her head to listen for any movement in the corridor. For all she knew, Greg had also posted guards outside this door. She didn't speak again until she was sure no one was listening in.

'Meryl, the police are here, coming for Greg.' She kept her voice low, eyes darting back to the door. 'It could get nasty. We have to get out before it kicks off or he could try using us to protect himself.'

Meryl frowned and pulled off one of her blankets, revealing her right arm, fastened by the wrist to the bed frame with something that thankfully didn't look like a handcuff. 'I don't see how we can.' She sighed, tugging at her restraint. 'That big muscle-bound idiot cable-tied me to the damn bed. I assume he did the same to you.'

Gloria shook her head. 'I got handcuffs, but I was hoping—'

She was cut off as the sound of a gunshot rang out from somewhere downstairs, leaving behind a painful silence which seemed to stretch on forever. Gloria and Meryl stared at each other through the gloom, wide-eyed and frozen in fear. Gloria's heart hammered against her ribs, and her mind started to race. She hadn't heard anyone break in, so the shot must have been fired from inside the house.

Greg.

Was he shooting at the police, at Hendrick? Her chest tightened as the worst possible scenario flashed in her mind.

Has he shot Iris?

She didn't want to wait to find out. She was getting out of here. Now.

Taking a deep breath, she braced her feet against the peeling wall, clenched her teeth and pulled, willing herself to block out the pain as her fragile skin grated against the cold metal handcuff. Unbidden groans escaped her lips as she felt her skin break, but she persevered. She squeezed her eyes shut to block out the pain, reminding herself that this was for Iris, and continued to heave until the cuff finally slipped over her fingers, clattering against the rusting metal of the radiator. The force almost knocked her onto her back, and she fell onto one elbow, her grazed hand already starting to throb.

Thank God!

There was no time to celebrate this small victory, however. Gloria scrambled to her feet and dashed over to the window, throwing back the curtains. She raised her hand to shield her eyes as the harsh glare of the streetlights bled in through the dirty glass.

'What can you see?' Meryl asked, squinting at the sudden influx of light.

'Nothing,' Gloria said, disappointed.

The window faced out onto a bare, concrete yard, seemingly devoid of activity. If the police were there, they were doing a very good job of keeping themselves hidden.

Or they're already inside the house.

CHAPTER THIRTY-NINE

'Meryl, we've got to get out. The police might be here already.'

'I told you, I'm tied!' Meryl tried to raise her arm and jerked as the cable tie around her wrist halted the movement. 'You go, get yourself somewhere safe. The police will come for me and let me out, I'm sure.'

They won't need to.

Gloria couldn't prevent her lips from curling into a small smile, and a look of confusion flashed across Meryl's bruised face. She dropped down to one knee and lifted her jeans up past her ankle, revealing a short kitchen knife, fixed to her leg with duct tape. It was the same knife Samuel and Katie had used to free Elias from his bindings, and Gloria had snatched it from the floor on impulse while preparing to meet Hendrick. She hadn't dared tell any of the others that she had it. Elias would never have allowed her to try sneaking it into the house without Greg finding it. It was reckless, but these were desperate times. They called for desperate measures.

'What on Earth is that doing there?' Meryl asked, aghast.

'This is *my* insurance policy.'

Gloria tore the blade from her skin, wincing as the tape ripped at her flesh. She pulled down the leg of her jeans and ran over to Meryl, quickly setting to work sawing through the plastic cable tying her to the bed. With a few short strokes, Meryl was freed. She threw the blankets onto the dusty floor and heaved herself off the bed, grimacing as she rotated her shoulder.

'That bloody cable tie has done a number on my rotator cuff. I'll be sending that brute a bill from my physiotherapist.'

Gloria held a finger up to her lips to signal for Meryl to be quiet, and together they crept towards the closed bedroom door. The house was too quiet; it was unnerving. The hairs rose on the back of Gloria's neck as she edged the door open a couple of inches to peer down the gloomy corridor. With the door ajar, she could hear some movement below, and the low buzz of muffled voices drifted up from downstairs. She strained to listen, but it was impossible to identify the speakers.

'Do you know how many men Greg has with him?' Gloria whispered, eyes darting up and down the empty corridor, expecting to see one of Greg's cronies appear at any moment. 'I only saw the stocky one by the door, and Elias said it was a group of three or four who took Iris.'

'They wouldn't speak to me when I asked questions,' Meryl was barely audible through her low whispers. 'But since I arrived, I've only seen the bully boy who brought me here and that little chap you mentioned. I gather Greg has quite the network, but with an ego that large he probably didn't think he needed many bodyguards overnight. Pride comes before a fall, let's hope.'

Gloria hoped to God Meryl was right. They might be able to slip past two or three distracted thugs, but she highly doubted they'd manage to fight through a whole team of them. She took a deep breath, drew her knife and prepared to move down the corridor. Her entire body thrummed with nervous energy. If she and Meryl ever had a realistic chance to escape, it was now.

'Let's go slow and quiet,' she whispered. 'If we see anyone, either we come back into the bedroom, or we hide in whichever room is closest. Hopefully, they'll be distracted as the police move in and we can get out without getting caught up in the crossfire. Sound good?'

Meryl smiled, eyes shining in the dim light. 'Yes, ma'am.'

Gloria was confused. 'Why are you smiling?'

'Crisis really brings out the best in you, Gloria. I'm impressed.'

Gloria returned the smile, an unfamiliar flutter of warmth spreading through her chest. It took her a second to realise it wasn't because of the praise she had just from Meryl, but because she was the one in charge. For the first time in years – perhaps even the first time ever – she was putting her fear to one side and taking matters into her own hands. She had control over her own destiny. And it felt good.

She nodded and led Meryl out into the corridor, listening hard for any unusual activity. They needed to tread carefully – these old townhouses were unstable and liable to creak under normal circumstances, and in their current situation, any unexpected movement would be heard across every floor. As they neared the staircase, the voices rising from downstairs started to become clearer, and Gloria could just about make out what they were saying.

'I swear, boss, there was someone out there. I saw him moving.' The voice was gruff and unfamiliar, lacking the well-spoken manner of Greg's typical associates. Gloria looked at

Meryl questioningly, but a shake of her head suggested this wasn't the tall thug who had brought her here.

'Well, who told you to fucking shoot?' Gloria's stomach clenched as Greg's voice pierced the air. 'I told you, check with me before you do *anything*. Whoever it was, you've scared them off now.'

They heard someone open the blinds to peer outside.

'Who would want to break into this dump, anyway?' Greg sneered.

'Maybe the big fella's trying to get in and take her back? He looked pissed off when you dragged her back in.'

Gloria's chest tightened.

Elias wouldn't risk it. Surely, he wouldn't?

Greg let out a sharp laugh. 'Unlikely. He might look like a tough guy, but he's as big a wimp as she is. They're like little birds, fluttering off at the slightest noise. Easy to scare, easier to control. It's foolproof.'

We'll see about that.

Gloria signalled to Meryl, and together they crept on towards the stairs. Gloria's heart hammered in her chest as they neared the top, her mouth growing drier with each step. *I should go first*, Gloria thought. *If we're caught, they can take it out on me, not Meryl.*

She lowered her foot onto the top step, ready to begin a careful descent. The old wood protested at the increased weight, letting out a piercing creak. Gloria froze in place, pulse racing. For a few seconds, there was silence, and she dared to hope the noise had gone unnoticed.

'What the hell was that?'

Gloria's stomach dropped to her feet, and she looked over at Meryl; her face had turned white.

'Charlie, go check upstairs and see if one of those bitches is messing about. Be quick about it.'

Gloria's eyes widened in panic. There was a limited choice of directions she could run, and none of the options would prevent Greg's thug from finding their room empty and raising the alarm. Then it would all be over.

They had to silence him somehow.

With no time to deliberate further, she signalled for Meryl to follow and dashed forwards past the stairs, through the only open door she could see. At the very least, she wasn't going to let them be caught like startled rabbits, frozen in the headlights of an oncoming car. They were going to put up a fight.

The door opened into a reasonably spacious bedroom which, judging by the familiar leather travel bag on the bed, must have been where Greg was staying. With any luck, this Charlie person wouldn't go snooping in his boss's bedroom. She and Meryl huddled behind the door so she could peer through the crack out onto the landing. The stairs groaned as the tall thug from earlier that day stomped up them, looking decidedly pissed off at being sent on another errand. Gloria couldn't help but smile as she noticed his shining black eye. Meryl had already given him a run for his money, it seemed.

'I hope the brute trips and breaks his neck,' Meryl whispered from behind Gloria, her voice full of distaste.

Gloria turned and looked at Meryl, whose eyes blazed with the same ferocity she could feel rising inside herself. 'Maybe he needs a nudge.'

A small, wicked smile crept across Meryl's lips. 'Let's do it.'

CHAPTER FORTY

Gloria clenched her fists, adrenaline pulsing through her body. Charlie was a lumbering, ogre-like man, but he would soon discover they had escaped their bindings and then there would be a very small window of opportunity in which to act. She watched with bated breath as he lazily strolled towards the room they had previously occupied, picking his nose.

He kicked the door open and stood in the doorway, visibly confused. As he ventured into the room, Gloria and Meryl tiptoed into the corridor and made their way towards the doorway as quietly as they could. Gloria halted for a moment to look down the stairs, half-expecting to see Greg staring up at her, anticipating her escape. A small twinge of relief passed over her as she saw nothing but the dusty old carpet, and she continued her careful steps to far side of the bedroom doorway, where Meryl awaited her.

Through the door, Gloria could hear the sounds of blankets, pillows and even furniture being thrown around the room as Charlie searched for the missing women. They pressed themselves into the wall, waiting, desperately hoping they wouldn't be noticed until it was much too late for Charlie.

'Shit!'

He was close to the door, and Gloria's heart jumped into her throat at the sound of his voice. She raised trembling hands, ready to thrust forward. She was aware of Meryl lowering herself down beside her, ready to kick out when needed. They were all set.

The bedroom door flung open, almost crashing into the two women. They glanced at each other, and Gloria nodded, her heart hammering in her chest.

Do it! We can't lose our nerve now.

Charlie stepped forward, gaze fixed ahead and oblivious to the two women only a foot or two to his left. Gloria jumped a little as he shouted downstairs, his thunderous voice echoing through the entire house. 'Boss! Boss! You've got to—'

Meryl kicked out her leg, hitting Charlie hard in the ankle with the heel of her boot. As he teetered forwards, Gloria lunged at him, slamming her open palms into his broad, muscular back with all her might. He stumbled, grasping hands reaching out for anything he could lay his hands on as gravity tugged at his massive weight. Gloria shrieked as his fingers closed around the hem of her blouse, his dirty nails digging into the soft fabric. He lurched forward and, for a terrifying moment, Gloria was going with him, pulled forward by his clinging grip.

She closed her eyes, bracing herself for the fall, but the weight dragging her onwards was suddenly released from her body, and she did nothing more than wobble at the top of the stairs. When she opened her eyes again, she saw Charlie crashing shoulder-first against the hardwood. There was no time for him to bring his hands up to protect himself, and his arm was forced behind his back with a sickening crack. Gloria wanted to look away, but her eyes remained fixed on the man as he barrelled onwards, his head and neck taking the force of his great weight as he collapsed in a mangled heap at the foot of the stairs, barely conscious.

Gloria wanted to celebrate the success of their manoeuvre, but in reality, all she could do was pity Charlie. He wasn't necessarily a bad man – he had just been doing what he was told, a monkey at the mercy of the organ grinder. For all she knew, he was full of remorse for what he had done, but badly needed the money. She would never know.

Gloria's musings were cut short as she heard the sound of urgent footsteps heading towards the bottom of the staircase, and a burst of anxiety bloomed in her stomach. Charlie's fall had made a spectacular racket, and their only chance of escape would be to get out before Greg understood what was happening.

She quickly tiptoed down the stairs, gesturing for Meryl to follow. Charlie's incapacitated body was sprawled across the old wooden floor at the bottom, quiet groans barely escaping his lips. Gloria's hands shook as she drew the kitchen knife, holding it ahead of herself, ready for whatever or whoever came at her. She had to get herself and Meryl out, whatever that took.

She prepared to step over Charlie, eyes darting left and right in search of Greg's approach. This wasn't a big house; if he wasn't there in the living room, he would be very soon. She didn't know the layout of the house, but there were likely only two options of escape: the front door to the right, or whatever lay beyond the doorway to the left.

'Charlie!'

Gloria's heart raced as Greg's voice reverberated around the empty ground floor.

'What the hell have you—?'

Greg stood in the doorway at the far left of the room, his eyes bulging with shock as he stared at the bottom of the stairs. His eyes moved between Charlie's body and the two women frozen at the foot of the stairs.

It was now or never.

Gloria prepared herself to make a dash for the front door, but before any of them could move an inch, a door burst open in the room behind Greg, and he spun around to see a small group of black-clad *Politie* filing into the room, shouting for him to get down.

CHAPTER FORTY-ONE

The next few minutes were nothing short of chaos.

Greg wasted no time before opening fire on the policemen, sending them scattering to the corners of the room, obscured by the interior wall. He backed up towards the stairs, shouting his own instructions to stand down. Gloria and Meryl's presence was temporarily forgotten as he tried to neutralise the current danger. His other bodyguard, the short man Gloria had seen by the door, was soon sprinting from the front of the house to join his boss, revolver in hand.

'What are you waiting for?' Greg snapped at him as they both hid behind the wall by the doorway. 'Get them out of here!'

The man hesitated for a moment, but under Greg's furious stare, he loaded his gun and lunged into the back room. Before his threat had begun to leave his mouth, he was hit with a bone-crunching punch to the face, sending him careering back into the living room. His gun skittered across the floor, slowing to a stop by Charlie's unmoving feet. Greg responded by firing at the offending officer, the bullet catching him in the arm and forcing him to retreat behind the safety of the wall.

Charlie stirred, head slowly turning towards the liberated firearm, but before he could make a move for it,

Gloria jumped over his body and kicked it across the room where it skidded and ricocheted off the front door, ending up somewhere under the front window. Greg's head span around and a pair of wild brown eyes met Gloria's for a moment, turning her blood cold.

They stood, eyes locked across the room, frozen together in the eye of the storm. Greg's body was rigid with tension, like a cobra poised to strike. Alarm bells rang in Gloria's head, urging her to run, but she couldn't leave Meryl behind, not after everything she'd done for her. Greg narrowed his eyes at his wife and moved as if to advance on her, but he was distracted as two *Politie* emerged from behind the wall, handguns pointed in his direction.

'Stand down!' one of them shouted with a loud, powerful voice. His face was obscured by his goggles and mouth covering, but Gloria's breath caught as she recognised him immediately.

Hendrick.

'Get back!' Greg shouted back as he raised his pistol, panic beginning to creep into his voice. 'Or I'll shoot every person in this room! That's a promise!'

It was a standoff. Greg's fallen comrade scrambled back to his feet, producing a small blade from his belt, forcing the policemen to divide their attention between the two threats. As the four men continued to shout threats back and forth, Gloria realised this was their opportunity.

'We have to get out while they're distracted,' she whispered, voice barely audible through the shouts. 'But we'll have to be as invisible as possible. You go first, quickly but quietly, to the front door. Don't look back. Once you're safely out, I'll go.'

Meryl nodded, and before Gloria could stop her, she pulled her into a tight embrace. Despite the noise and chaos swirling around them, and the very real danger she knew they were in, Gloria held on to her friend for as long as she could, not wanting to let go. She had been so relieved to be reunited with Meryl again, to know she was safe, and her heart ached as she released her from her arms. Meryl looked up at her, kind eyes shining with the threat of tears.

'You come as soon as I'm clear, you hear?' she said softly, gripping Gloria's hands tightly in her own. 'Be careful, please.'

With that, she kissed Gloria lightly on the cheek, span on her heel and headed towards the front door, stepping lightly on the balls of her feet. She glanced over her shoulder at the men at the other end of the room, ensuring they were thoroughly distracted before turning the key and slipping outside. As she disappeared through the door, Gloria prepared to make her own break for it, but she was unable to resist taking one last look towards the man she once loved, now locked in a shouting match with Hendrick and his companion. From the corner of her eye, she noticed another officer emerging through the doorway a few feet behind them.

Gloria froze as her eyes zeroed in on the newcomer. Unlike the others, he wore nothing to cover his head or face, revealing shaggy blond hair and piercing blue eyes.

Elias! What are you doing in here?

His eyes scanned the room, locking with Gloria's for one electrifying moment before he turned to face Greg. Gloria's voice screamed inside her head to run, to follow the plan and get out of that house whilst she had the chance, but her body wouldn't listen. Despite her shrieking inner protestations, her feet drew her closer to the standoff, towards the two most significant men in her life.

Hendrick glanced away from Greg as Elias approached, and his eyes bulged in recognition. He waved and shouted for Elias to get back, but he didn't listen. He moved forwards, slowly advancing on Greg, unblinking eyes blazing with fury.

Greg shifted his gaze from Hendrick, acknowledgement flashing in his eyes as they settled on Elias. Gloria's stomach tightened as a sickening smirk grew on his lips. He redirected his aim, and before Gloria knew what she was doing, she had lunged forwards, racing towards a loaded pistol.

'NO!' she screamed as she pushed Greg's arm upwards, the sound of a shot piercing the air as she did.

A cry of pain rang out, and Gloria realised she still had the knife in her hand. For a moment she thought she must have stabbed Greg in the arm, but as she looked down, she saw the blade was clean; she had done nothing more than slash his jacket sleeve open, exposing the pristine white shirt beneath.

Heart racing, she spun around and plunged the knife towards Greg's body, but it was too late; he'd had all the time he needed to react. The room became a blur as he snatched Gloria's arm and twisted it behind her back. His other hand wrenched the knife from her desperate fingers. She heard it clatter against the floor as Greg tossed it across the room, jerking her back to press her against his body. She had unwittingly offered herself as a human shield. Again.

Wait.

If it wasn't Greg who was in pain, then who—

A soft groan drew her attention, and she stared through hot, angry tears as Elias collapsed to the floor in front of her.

CHAPTER FORTY-TWO

'We need a medic!' Hendrick shouted into his radio, kneeling to place a hand on Elias's chest, his shirt already slick with blood. 'Quickly!'

He pointed his gun back up at Greg, and Gloria flinched, painfully aware she was now in the firing line. 'Don't move!'

Greg responded with a laugh so savage it made Gloria's skin crawl.

'The ball is in my court now, copper.' He pressed his pistol into the back of Gloria's skull, forcing her head forwards so she could see only the grimy floorboards, already spattered with Elias's fresh blood. She tried to tug her arm free, but Greg was holding her against him with an iron grip. There was no escape.

'Make one more move towards me, and I'll blow her fucking head off.'

'Don't do this, Greg.' Hendrick sounded calm, but his wide eyes betrayed him, revealing his panic. 'We've got the house surrounded. There's nowhere to go.'

Greg backed towards the front of the house, dragging Gloria along with him. She could see nothing but her own feet and stumbled as she tried to keep up, falling and scraping her knee against the old, splintered floor.

'You expect me to believe that crap? We've been watching the windows – there's no one outside.'

'I have men stationed all around this building. You've got nowhere to go.'

'Bullshit!' His voice was rising, and panic flooded Gloria's body. She could feel the gun shaking as Greg pressed it harder against her skull.

He's losing control, and he knows it.

'You've already shot one civilian, Greg. Do you really want to go down for shooting two?'

'Shut up!' Greg shouted, dragging Gloria further. 'We're going. Do not follow us, or else.'

We'll be at the front door any second, Gloria thought, her heart sinking. He was going to get his way after all, like he always did.

Greg pulled her to a stop and pushed the gun so hard into Gloria's head, she was forced to kneel in front of him. A surge of adrenaline pulsed through her body, urging her to run, but she couldn't move. She was paralysed with fear.

'Don't move,' he whispered into her ear, his hot breath sending a shiver down her spine.

Gloria heard him take several slow steps backwards. As she heard him fumble with the door handle, she knelt frozen in place, too terrified to even lift her head to see what was happening around her. The skin between her shoulder blades itched as she pictured the hand gun she was certain was still pointed directly at her. Fresh tears welled in her eyes, and she did nothing to prevent them from falling onto the dusty wooden floorboards.

God, when will this end?

When the front door finally swung inwards, the room was bathed in flashing blue light. Gloria expected to find it reassuring, but it was anything but. Greg now knew his chances of escape were dwindling. Perhaps he wouldn't need a human shield, after all. She was now disposable.

'Shit!' Greg muttered. Within seconds, Gloria once again felt the pressure of cold, hard steel against her skull.

'I told you.' Hendrick's voice was slow and careful.

He knows Greg's getting desperate.

'You're surrounded. Give up now, and no one else needs to get hurt.'

God, please, let him listen.

'No.' Greg's voice rose with each word; he was verging on hysterical. 'No! This isn't over!'

Gloria felt his powerful hand rake through her hair, and he raised her up, her scalp screaming as her entire body weight was lifted into the air until his face was only inches away from hers.

'Is this what you wanted?' he spat, shaking her so violently she felt her teeth rattling in her gums. 'Is it?'

Gloria shrank away as Greg sprayed her with angry saliva, his face contorted with rage.

'You could have had everything! You had no good reason to leave!'

Gloria knew she should keep quiet and accept his tirade – he could kill her at any moment. But she couldn't stay silent, not anymore.

Enough is enough.

'No.' Her voice was quiet but firm. 'What you did was wrong, Greg. You had no right!'

'Wrong?' He raised her up higher, and Gloria couldn't hold back a shriek of pain as her hair began to tear from her scalp. 'What was wrong was me thinking a cheap, common slut like you could be brought back into civilised society. You started as scum, and you always will be scum!'

'Your words mean nothing to me,' Gloria spat back, a triumphant smile curling at the edges of her mouth. 'You don't own me anymore.'

Greg threw her face-down onto the floorboards and flashes of pain shot up her arms as her elbows slammed into the hardwood.

'We'll see about that.'

Gloria rose to her knees and lifted her head, freezing in place as she felt the cold barrel of the pistol once again.

'You are mine, Gloria. You hear that? Mine!'

His hands were trembling violently now, the gun rattling against the back of Gloria's skull as he pressed down harder.

'If I can't have you, nobody can!'

Gloria squeezed her eyes shut, hot tears streaming down her cheeks. It was too late; she knew that. She had said too much. *I don't regret a thing,* she thought, bracing for the end. *At least it ends on my terms, not his.*

Her entire body recoiled as a single shot was fired, sending an explosion of sound tearing through her eardrums.

Silence followed, broken only by a faint, high-pitched ringing in both of her ears.

But she felt nothing.

What's happening? Am I dead?

Gloria finally opened her eyes as she felt the pressure of the revolver disappear from the back of her head. There was the sound of a dull thud behind her as something heavy crashed to the ground. She could barely breathe. How was she still alive?

Trembling all over, she slowly turned to look behind her and gasped at what she saw, bile rising to the back of her throat. There, sprawled across the floorboards, blood pooling around his head, was Greg.

Dead.

Gloria slowly lifted her head, and she almost collapsed herself as she laid her eyes on the figure standing in the doorway, silhouetted against the glare of the blue lights, a pistol smoking in her shaking hands.

'Iris?'

CHAPTER FORTY-THREE

The darkening Amsterdam sky was streaked with bands of warm amber, its glittering reflection rippling in the calm canal waters below, giving the view an ethereal quality. Despite the evening drawing in, the street was peppered with people rushing about their business, filling the city with life. It buzzed with a peculiar energy that was difficult to place.

Perhaps it was hope.

A warm breeze fluttered through the window, stirring the curtains and embracing Gloria in sublime serenity. She closed her eyes, feeling a peace she was certain she had never experienced before.

'The sky is beautiful tonight.'

Her eyes fluttered open, and she turned to see Elias, his warm face smiling broadly, his bright blue eyes glittering in the soft light shining through the window.

'You should be resting.' Gloria raised her eyebrows, eyeing the sling cradling his injured shoulder.

'But I come bearing gifts!' He winked, holding out a steaming mug of tea with his good arm, which Gloria accepted gratefully. It smelled faintly of cinnamon and vanilla, the creamy, warm aromas filling her nostrils and tickling her taste buds.

'My favourite.' She smiled up at him, butterflies stirring in her stomach. 'What did I do to deserve this treat?'

'It wasn't entirely selfless.' He grinned, stepping aside and gesturing towards the centre of the room, where Iris sat on the small sofa, smiling up at them both from under a blanket and clutching a large bowl of popcorn. '*Someone* wants a family movie night.'

'Ah.' She took a long sip from her mug, delighting in the comforting heat of the fragrant liquid before handing it back to Elias. 'Well, in that case, save me a seat, and I'll pack up my brushes and join you.'

Elias leaned forwards and planted a soft kiss on Gloria's cheek, sending a pleasant shiver running down her body. He walked back to join Iris on the sofa, which sparked some light-hearted bickering over which film they would watch. It wasn't long before it escalated into a full-blown tickle-fight, with Iris using her dad's injury to her full advantage in order to orchestrate her escape into the kitchen.

Gloria's heart swelled with pride as she watched her daughter, finally able to smile and laugh again after weeks of counselling. Iris had saved her life, perhaps all of their lives. It would be a long time before she recovered from her ordeal, but she was strong, and Gloria would make sure she got all the help she needed. Gloria owed her everything, and would always be grateful to her. And to Hendrick, of course, for smoothing everything over with his bosses afterwards. He had been true to his promise, protecting Iris as he had once protected Gloria at that age, and she was sure it would continue. She smiled as she thought of not only Hendrick, but also Katie, Meryl and Samuel. With Greg, she had felt alone; friendless. She hadn't realised it at the time, but the solitude was tearing her apart. Now, she knew she had the best friends anyone could ever ask for. She felt truly blessed.

GLORIA

Gloria began wiping off her brushes, happy for the day's painting to be cut short under the circumstances. It was no longer a desperate escape from reality. It was a joy, complimented perfectly by the other loves of her life.

Well, it will be. After tomorrow.

Gloria wasn't looking forward to her meeting with the press to blow the lid off Genisolve's unsavoury underbelly, but she had to make sure no one else would suffer like she and Iris had. She could do that much, at least. That wasn't a worry for this evening, though. For now, she pulled the window closed and drew the curtains, turning away from the beautiful sunset to take in a much more spectacular view – her family, and her home.

Sometimes it takes going through the very worst for your eyes to finally open and let you see that you had what you needed all along.

This was love. It may not be perfect, but it was real, and that's all she really wanted.

ACKNOWLEDGEMENTS

Before I get into the personal acknowledgements, I'd like to thank the father and daughter I passed while walking along the riverbank, back when Gloria was still just an idea in my head. You became Elias and Iris, and in that moment you made this story what it is today.

Firstly, I'd like to thank my family, who have always believed in me, even when I didn't believe in myself. Special thanks go to my mum, for drilling correct grammar into my brain as a child and always being a thorough and effective proof-reader of my work. A huge thank you to my sister Brontë, whose amazing cover artwork exceeded my expectations. You always know how to make my incoherent ideas come to life.

A novel is never written in a single draft, so thank you to my talented editor Vicky Brewster, who helped make my manuscript shine. I'm also grateful to my enthusiastic friends and beta readers Rachel, Hannah and Georgia – your feedback was invaluable and your enthusiasm for Gloria and her story meant so much to me.

I wouldn't be where I am today if it wasn't for the online writing community. You know who you are, and without all of your advice, support and encouragement, I'd still be floundering.

Finally, thank you to my husband, Ryan, who always has absolute faith in me. You were there to give me that extra push when I was too scared to take the plunge, and I'll forever be grateful for that.

THANK YOU FOR READING

Readers of Gloria are eligible for an exclusive free copy of my short story

BROKEN LEGACY

Go to katherineshawwrites.com/freeshortstory to claim your copy now!

ABOUT THE AUTHOR

Katherine Shaw is a Yorkshire-born multi-genre writer of both long and short-form fiction, based in a little fisherman's cottage on the bank of the Humber Estuary.

Despite being a chemist by training, she has been a writer ever since she could pick up a pencil, and feels she was born with an innate need to write stories. Her parents still ask her about the fantasy series she was dreaming up as a child on the beach during a family holiday at Bournemouth.

When she isn't working or daydreaming about new characters, Katherine is an avid Dungeons and Dragons player (and fledgling DM), a reader of all genres, a mediocre choir singer, a lover of daily yoga practice, and a player of vintage video games. Some may say that she's a geek...

GLORIA is Katherine's debut novel. Connect with her online to keep up to date with the launch of her next release.

Twitter @katheroony
Instagram @katherineshawwrites
facebook.com/katherineshawwrites
www.katherineshawwrites.com